The Knife With Eyes

The Knife
With Eyes

Dayle Courtney

**Illustrated by
John Ham**

STANDARD PUBLISHING
Cincinnati, Ohio   2716

Thorne Twins Adventure Books

Library of Congress Cataloging in Publication Data

Courtney, Dayle.
  The knife with eyes.

  (Thorne Twins adventure books ; 3)
  Summary: Searching for a rare art form on the Isle of Skye
in Scotland, sixteen-year-old Alison and her twin, with their
Christian values, uncover a plot involving espionage and
revenge.
  [1. Mystery and detective stories. 2. Christian life—Fiction.
3. Twins—Fiction] I. Ham, John. II. Title. III. Series:
Courtney, Dayle. Thorne Twins adventure books ; 3.
PZ7.C83158Kn   [Fic]   81-5624
ISBN O-87239-471-9   AACR2

Contents

Long Before...

Only madmen travel in that season. February—in Siberia—the month of storms. In that land the distances are so great, the inhabitants say, that only the
archangel Michael has measured them. Covered with
storm-carved drifts of snow, the land stretches with
a heart-numbing impassiveness from horizon to horizon, broken only by the dark reaches of the nearly
impenetrable forests.

Trees in these forests sometimes burst into flames,
struck by lightning or ignited by the friction of the
branches rubbing against each other in the unrelenting
Arctic wind. The sap and needles burn like a huge torch
set by some unknown hand in the night—a signal that
no eye will see in this void—before the snow melting
from the canopy of interlacing branches above ex-
tinguishes the flames. These charred corpses remain
long after the roots die, standing like black slash

marks against the deep spaces, as though the hand that had set the fires had then tried to cancel the desolate scene out of existence.

Even the moon looked glacial against the gray sky. From the dark woods plunged a troika, the whip-driven animals harnessed to it panting as they raced, their tongues lolling from the sides of their mouths. Again and again the driver brought his whip down against their backs. His passenger sat behind, covered against the cold by a thick fur *malitsa*.

Only someone maddened by living too long, exposed to this harsh and friendless area, would risk being caught in one of the storms that suddenly rake the Siberian landscape in late winter. Caught in such a storm the land's vast distances are reduced to nothing but white as the horizon disappears, obscured by the masses of snow whipping against the eye.

The driver of the troika, his face reddened by the cold, and his unkempt beard flecked with crystals of snow, looked over his shoulder at the passenger.

"We should have come the other way!" he shouted over the rush of wind. "Along the Sosva. The snow's still too heavy here in the mountains."

The passenger's gaze leveled on the driver was as deadly as a rifle's gunsights.

"The route by the river is twice as long," said the passenger. "That would give the soldiers twice as much time to catch up with us. It's this route or none."

In the early years of the Revolution, a few political prisoners had escaped, following the same paths as those who had fled from Tsar's guards. South, retracing the great Tobolsk road that had brought them to the prison camps. Or east across the Urals and then to Archangel by way of Izhma, there to wait for the icebound harbor to thaw in the spring and a foreign ship to smuggle aboard. Or west, the direction in which the troika was dashing: towards the Ural ore mines, the narrow gauge railway to Bogoslovsk, then the Kotlass-Perm line. To Vyatka, Volgda beyond that, then to Finland and freedom. Failure at any one of these points meant death, trapped on the snowbound trail. Or a bullet in the back from a soldier's rifle.

An Ostyak tent village appeared ahead beside the trail. "We must stop for a bit," the driver called to the passenger. "To rest the animals."

The passenger said nothing: he could see for himself the stumbling gait and sharp, laboring breaths of the tormented beasts.

The driver brought the troika up beside the largest of the huddled group of yurts. An acrid odor of smoke touched the passenger's nostrils. A muted gabble of voices could be heard from inside the yurt.

"I must thaw myself," said the driver, dismounting. "My hands—so frozen—barely grip the reins."

He lifted his hands to demonstrate it was impossible to flex the stiff leather gloves. His reindeer-skin boots crunched through the muddy snow as he staggered to the yurt, where he pushed aside the leather flap over the door and entered.

"*Paisi, paisi!*" welcomed his entrance.

The passenger waiting in the troika had no wish for human company. The cramped conditions of a prison barracks had cured him of that. He sat watching the moon's pallid light slide across the massed banks of snow. His face showed little but the hollowed cheeks and dark eye sockets. Behind that mask was a driving hunger greater than that of the body.

Half an hour passed and the driver had not emerged. The passenger threw aside the *malitsa* and stepped down from the troika. He made his way toward the yurt, slowed by a dragging limp in his right leg. The foot turned inward with each step, the sign of a broken bone improperly set or—given the harsh conditions of a prison camp—not set at all.

Pulling aside the flap of skin from across the doorway, he peered into the yurt's recesses.

Through the air made thick with the central fire's grease-laden smoke, he saw the driver sharing a story with a group of Ostyaks. Sullen Mongol faces, with dark plaits of hair dangling behind, turned toward the intruder. They squinted to pierce the haze and fumes of alcohol in their heads.

The passenger looked only at the driver. "Outside," he ordered. "And to your reins. We have many *versts* yet to go."

"The road's snowbound," the driver sneered. "They've told me so. No one's going anywhere."

"We are. You've got my money in your pocket. I didn't pay you to dump me here for the soldiers to come and pick up at their convenience."

10

The driver grunted, but made no sign of getting up.

"Maybe I can offer you something more in order to change your mind," the passenger said as he grabbed the front of the driver's shirt and pulled him to his feet. Before he could form any resistance, the limping man was dragging him from the yurt.

"Here," said the passenger, pushing the driver against the side of the troika. "I didn't bring much with me, but—"

With one hand he pushed the driver's face toward the seat; with the other he opened a small leather sack that had been stored beneath it. Ostyak faces peered out from the doorway of the yurt.

Suddenly, the driver cried out and stumbled back from the troika. Rivulets of blood seeped from between the fingers of his hand clutched to his face. Drops spattered onto the snow and froze into small round gems.

"Take it!" screamed the driver, his other hand jerking toward the troika. "And the animals! Just go, and take your devil with you!"

"Very well," the passenger said closing the sack and pushing it back beneath the seat. He mounted and took up the reins. The animals stood and waited, pawing the ground. The noisy Ostyaks were suddenly silent as they gaped at the scene before them.

"You'll die!" howled the driver in pain and fear, his bloody hand clamped to his face. "You don't know the way! The road's snowbound! You'll die and be buried in the snow!"

"I won't die," said the other simply. "I can't die—not yet." Then he was gone, onto the narrow road and into the dark forests beyond.

Just Before...

The clanging roar of the Manhattan traffic faded as the thick glass doors closed silently. No sound came as their pneumatic cylinders latched into place. A magnetic locking device kept out all intruders who lacked a coded passkey with electronic triggering impulses implanted along its length.

The security guard glanced up from his desk station as the man crossed the lobby. A small amber light on the control panel had flicked on when the door had opened. Each of the electronic passkeys had an additional coding that identified which tenant had entered.

APT. 18 NORTH—MARTIN read the tag beside the amber light.

A brief look was all it took to assure the security guard that the passkey had been used by its rightful owner. It usually required several weeks for the guards to familiarize themselves with a new tenant's face—

13

there were so many inhabitants of the high rise, a virtual city in itself, that it was easy to lose track—but this man had engraved a permanent impression on all the staff's minds within a week of his moving in.

What it was that made the man so striking was difficult to put into words. He was an older man, perhaps in his seventies, but still bearing his thin frame erect. He was dressed in a well-cut gray suit that spoke of money—nothing unusual in this building, a haven for the rich and powerful.

It was the man's infirmity that stayed in one's memory. He had a pronounced limp, the right foot twisting inward and dragging as the man supported his steps with a thin black cane topped with a discreet silver knob. Somehow his face seemed disconnected from the rest of his body—the labored difficulty of his motion did not register on the grave, sharp-angled features that seemed carved into higher relief by more than the passage of years. Some type of emotional force greater than hunger had cut into the hollows of the old man's face, perhaps long before, and never left.

The building's lobby was a sanctuary of peace and quiet, the kind of refuge from the harsh world outside that only money could bring. Money, and the fear of losing it, provided the magnetic door locks, the 24-hour security guards, the video cameras scanning the plush carpeted hallways. The guard turned from the limping man to the rows of monitor screens behind the high counter of his station. Nothing was amiss

14

anywhere in the building: the screens or the alarms would have indicated it if it were.

The limping man crossed the lobby to the elevator doors and stood waiting with another tenant already there. The numbers above the doors blinked a slow countdown as the elevator descended. The man with the limp, his brown-spotted hands folded on the head of his cane, nodded courteously as his fellow tenant glanced up from his copy of the *Wall Street Journal*.

It was no more than a slight tilting of the head, but it meant, yes, we do not know each other, but we are the same: we inhabit the same world of money and privilege.

The man returned Martin's nod and went back to his newspaper, awaiting the elevator's arrival. But somehow he couldn't concentrate on the printed words. Something about the limping man's face stirred in the recesses of his mind, rousing confused, buried memories. The man was obviously a new tenant, but where had he seen that seamed, angular face before?

"Excuse me—"

The resident of Apartment 18 North leaned his cane against the wall and was reaching into his coat pocket.

"I noticed the initials on your briefcase," he said. The voice was polite and reserved, with a trace of some unidentifiable accent. "I wonder if this perhaps belongs to you."

He held a small object out on his palm.

Involuntarily, the man with the newspaper glanced at the briefcase at his feet, then at the object in the limping man's hand. The letters L R S were on both.

"I—I believe it is mine," he said, surprised. He took the heavy silver cuff link with the small blue-white diamond lettering and held it to the light.

"Why—yes, it is. I had the set custom made a few years ago. But where—?"

He stared at the man beside him.

"I found it here," the limping man said simply. "In the elevator. It must have fallen from your shirt cuff when you returned from wherever you wore them last. Naturally, I intended to turn it over to the security guard, but fortunately I've now been able to save you the trouble of inquiring for it." He smiled gravely.

"Well—thank you. Yes, thanks." The other man struggled to gain control of the growing confusion inside himself. "It was very, uh, kind of you, Mr.— I'm sorry, but I don't know your name."

"Martin," said the limping man.

"Mine's Strother. That's what the *S* stands for, of course." He laughed nervously.

"That's an excellent piece of jewelry, Mr. Strother. The stones especially are of a very fine water."

"Oh? Are you a connoisseur of gems?"

"I deal in diamonds," said the limping man. "And other commodities."

The elevator doors slid open. Strother slipped the cuff link into his pocket, picked up his briefcase, and with his other hand reached out and held the elevator doors from sliding shut again.

"Going up, Mr. Martin?" he asked, searching the

man's angular face for a clue from his memory.

"No," the other said, shaking his head. His eyes had narrowed into slits as his face had become even paler, almost bloodless. "I've changed my mind. I think I'll go outside for some air."

"Well, thanks again." Puzzled, Strother stepped into the elevator and let the doors close, shutting off the figure of the limping man crossing the lobby, the point of his cane probing the deep carpeting.

The questions grew larger and more insistent in Strother's mind all the way to the twentieth floor. He unlocked the door of his apartment and strode back to the bedroom. Pawing through the articles on the tortoise shell tray on his dresser, he found the mate to the returned cuff link and stared at the pair of them.

I haven't worn these links for at least two months! he thought. *I couldn't have returned one to the tray and not have noticed the other was missing.*

He was no fool. He knew that the brilliant assemblage of silver and diamonds like points of light could not have lain in the elevator all these months without being picked up by one of the cleaning ladies or another tenant. The whole thing was impossible to believe!

He stepped to the phone beside the bed and dialed the security desk downstairs.

"This is Mr. Strother on the twentieth. I want the locksmith and the electronics systems man up here, and I want them immediately. I don't care if it is after

18

five. I'll pay the overtime. Just get them here." He slammed the phone down and waited.

Less than an hour later, he had the experts' receipts in his hand and their diagnoses: None of the door locks showed any signs of having been tampered with, and the alarm systems were all fully operative. No one could have gotten in without his permission.

He lay on his bed as the daylight faded; his thoughts passing slowly, obsessively through the unanswered questions in his head. Gradually, the mystery of how the diamond-studded cuff link had traveled from his dresser to the enigmatic Mr. Martin's pocket receded as the more insistent mystery repeated itself louder and louder.

"Where have I seen that limping man before?"

Some time after the room was completely dark, a connection fell into place in his memory. Years melted away, and he saw Martin's face, younger and unmarked by that deep cutting hunger. Strother's spine contracted into a solid rod as he realized who it was.

The phone rang. Without turning on the lamp, he reached out and picked it up.

"Good evening, Strother." The voice on the other end was mocking, transforming the name into a shallow alias.

Strother pushed his voice through his tightening throat. "What do you want?"

"You don't know? I should think you'd be able to guess, just from the fact that I'm still alive. And the fact that I found you."

19

"That—that—all that was a long time ago."

"Not for me," the voice on the other end said evenly. "It seems like yesterday to me."

"I had to do what I did," he pleaded. "There was my family—my wife and my little girl. I had to protect them!"

"I had a family, also." Martin's voice hardened. "Where are they now?"

Silence.

Strother's breathing became faster, racing with his heartbeat. "How—did you get in here?"

"I didn't." The line clicked as the connection was broken.

For a moment, panic kept him paralyzed on the bed. Then he scrambled to his feet and raced to his front door. He checked the locks against their steel surfaces fumbling in his sweating fingers. He was literally panting with fear as he ran through the apartment, switching on all the lights.

He stopped finally in the middle of the living room, a carving knife from one of the kitchen drawers clutched in his hand.

What is there to be afraid of? he said to himself, struggling for control. *Nothing but an old man—*

"I'm imagining things," he muttered, taking a firmer hold of the carving knife. "There's nothing but an old man somewhere in his own apartment in the building, with no way to hurt me. The trick with the cuff link can be explained somehow. There's no way he can get to me."

Just then he saw two yellow points of light glimmering in the darkness under the sofa. He bent over to see what it was.

The doors were still locked and all the lights were on the next day when a security guard who had failed to get an answer found him. A brown stain surrounded Strother's head where he lay face down on the carpet. Two small but deep cuts on the victim's throat, precise as from a surgical knife, were all the coroner found.

1 • Castles in the Air

A gray November sky hung over Washington D.C.

Clouds the color of steel scudded overhead in the sharp wind that made the leafless branches of the city's trees tremble.

With his shoulders hunched forward and his hands jammed into his coat pockets, the energy coiled in Eric Thorne's well-knit sixteen-year-old frame propelled his long legs automatically over the sidewalks. The wind brought a spot of color to his face. The vacant gaze in his eyes showed how far he was lost in his thoughts as he walked along. Two men followed him a half block behind.

Eric knew it was going to be different after the election, but he hadn't realized how much. For one thing, his grandfather was now Vice President of the United States. That accounted for the two Secret Service agents with dark gray suits who followed him everywhere. They had been assigned to him right after an incident out in Hollywood and, almost as an afterthought, another pair had been detailed to his twin sister.

Alison had adjusted more quickly.

"Good old Alison," Eric muttered into his upturned collar. "She seems to have a special talent for doing the right thing and keeping out of trouble. Off she goes, her camera and tote bag slung over her shoulder, her two agents trailing behind her just as if nothing had changed at all!"

But everything *had* changed.

Eric envied his sister—his own mind seemed so mixed-up and confused. For the first time in his life he wondered if there was anything that he could get involved in with as much satisfaction as Alison got out of her photography—not to mention her music.

As far as his own Secret Service agents were concerned, after he accepted their presence, he discovered he actually liked them. A couple of times he went along with them to fire off a few practice rounds in the FBI building's basement shooting range. Eric smiled to himself as he remembered how surrised they had been at the way he handled a weapon. Like a lot of kids growing up in the Midwest, Eric had a good deal of practice hunting with a rifle.

"You ought to be protecting *us*," the agents had joked. In some ways, Eric felt he'd miss the two of them, now that the election was over and they were due to be reassigned.

He saw them out of the corner of his eye as he turned into his grandfather's law offices.

There was a distinct morning-after-the-election feeling about the place.

The election, voting returns, network broadcasts, and the big victory celebration for his grandfather and the President-elect were all over now, and all that remained was a muddle of confetti and paper streamers. Eric didn't recognize half the people scurrying about, packing away the contents of the file cabinets, boxing up his grandfather's books, cleaning out his desk, getting ready for the big move.

Standing in the middle of all the commotion was Mary Johnson, directing the action with a clipboard baton, checking off the contents of files as they were tucked into the cardboard transport boxes.

"Eric!" called Mary, spotting him at the edge of the office. She motioned him over with her clipboard.

"Hi," he said after he threaded his way through the clutter. "How's it going?"

"Chaos," she answered, tucking a straggling lock back behind her ear. "Complete *chaos*. Believe me, it's not defeat that's hard—it's what comes after winning that'll break your back."

Eric smiled at her, knowing that her exasperation was half in jest. She'd been working for his grandfather ever since he had been in the Senate. She had stuck by him through everything, and now she was going to be the executive secretary for the Vice President of the whole USA!

25

"Everything," she continued, "has to be boxed up and moved over to your grandfather's office at party headquarters. Then in January, after the Inauguration, it all has to be moved *again*!"

"Why move it twice?" asked Eric.

"Oh—possible conflict of interest," she said with a touch of annoyance. "Your grandfather's law partners—former partners, that is—can't very well have the next Vice President right in their offices with them. At least not in Washington, D.C., they can't."

She laid her hand on his shoulder and peered over the top of her half-rimmed glasses at him. "But anyway, what I wanted to tell you is that the luncheon has been canceled. The conference about the cabinet nominations was moved forward and is expected to go on for a while. There's a lot to be done."

Mary saw the disappointment in his face. "Eric," she said softly, "he's Vice President Thorne first now, and your grandfather second."

"Well, sure," he said, shrugging. "I mean, that's what we all worked for, isn't it?" He said good-bye to her and made his way out of the crowded office.

A few minutes later, Eric let himself into his grandparents' townhouse. The gracious residence in Washington, D.C. was as much their home as their father's house back in Ivy, Illinois. He went upstairs and found Alison.

She was sitting cross-legged on her bed, surrounded by opened magazines and books, and poring over a large map spread out in front of her.

"Hi," she said, glancing up and catching sight of Eric in the doorway of her room. "Mrs. Johnson called—"

"Yeah, I know, the luncheon's been canceled. We all get the afternoon off."

He sat on the corner of the bed and glanced idly around her room. Alison had never gone for the frills and flounces most girls loved. Her way of decorating a room was to have her various projects and interests piled about her. Right now a camera tripod was planted in a pile of sheet music. One wall was covered with election posters. Another displayed the black-and-white photographs she had taken during the campaign. A few had resisted the tacks, and were curled like scrolls. On an easel was a layout of Richard Avedon's portrait photography.

"Eric," said Alison in a low, mock-conspiratorial whisper, "What are you planning on doing now?"

"Oh, I don't know. Maybe go to the gym."

"No, silly, not what are you planning to do this afternoon. I mean *now*. Now that the campaign and the election and all that are over. What do you want to do *now*?"

"I'm not ready for a question like that," he told her with a grimace. "I haven't really thought about it. Other than just getting back to school again, I guess. So what's on *your* mind?"

Alison smiled and raised the map for him to see. "Going to Scotland," she announced, still in a mood of conspiracy.

All his life, he and Alison had been on the same wavelength—almost telepathic. Not like some twins he knew who shared the same genetic material, but whose minds were on quite different tracks. This time, however, Alison's plans caught him flat-footed.

"Scotland?" he said. "What brought this on? What's in Scotland? I mean besides the Loch Ness monster? Let me guess—you want to photograph it!"

"Don't be ridiculous, Eric. I do have some serious thoughts once in a while. In fact, that's exactly the point. I, for one, would like to go back to Central High and be credited for something besides being the Vice President's granddaughter."

Alison rummaged through the clutter around her as though looking for the evidence to drive home her point.

"Here," she said, pulling a magazine from the confusion, "you could stand a fresh image yourself!"

It was a low blow.

Alison was brandishing a copy of *Faces* magazine, the publication most responsible for Eric's problems in California.

Faces had been the first to play up all the things that a certain bubble-headed actress had said about Eric at a Hollywood fund-raiser. Then a couple of weeks later the gossipy magazine had put him on their cover, with a lot of nonsense inside about him being a "hot young Hollywood hopeful" with dreams about starring in a couple of movies and a television special. His embarrassment had known no bounds when he'd seen how they had misquoted him. After that, he was mobbed by teenagers when he had been with his grandfather who had spoken at a dinner in Denver. Following this event, the Secret Service agents had been assigned to him and to his sister. Things hadn't seemed normal since. Eric Thorne did not enjoy being a "celebrity."

Eric wondered if his sister was still holding an angry grudge against *Faces* magazine. Compared to the copy and pictures they had printed about him, there had been only one small photo of her. The magazine seemed to convey that having a twin sister was just another interesting thing about *him*. They had even described her as "plain but bright," which made them both furious. They had the same brown eyes, wide forehead, and high cheekbones that came from a trace of Indian blood on their mother's side.

"If the magazine thought it all looked so good on you, Eric, why not on me?" Alison had fumed.

"I'd give anything if I didn't have to see or hear about that piece of trash again!" Eric said angrily, grabbing the offending magazine and throwing it against the wall. You think *you* need something to support your reentry to the halls of Central High? What about me? I cringe when I think what some of those guys—"

"Say no more, brother dear! With that admission you have made yourself a full partner in a scheme that will get both of us back on track. You ought to know I wouldn't plan a trip to Scotland without you."

His twin's efficiency had always impressed him, and no more than now. Eric listened as she told him about their next semester's subjects. What interested her especially were the texts assigned for literature.

"We're going to study two of Tolstoy's works," Alison announced excitedly. "*War and Peace* and *Anna Karenina*!"

"So—" Eric commented, wondering what that could have to do with Scotland.

"Well, by the oddest coincidence, I just read about this Russian concert pianist who defected to Scotland a long time ago—"

Alison paused to dig around for another magazine in the clutter on her bed. It was a journal on the performing arts, and she opened it before her puzzled brother.

"This woman—she's retired now—said in an interview after her last concert that her father actually *knew* Tolstoy. More than that, she has in her possession some unpublished notations and letters Tolstoy wrote to her father about his work!"

"I still don't know what all this has to do with Scotland," Eric said drily.

"Didn't I tell you? She now lives on the Isle of Skye!"

The article Alison showed Eric was illustrated with the photo of a woman, gray-haired, her expressive face sharpened with age. The photo puzzled him. It had a grainy quality to it, as if it had been magnified several times.

"Who is she?" he asked.

"Oh, her name's Anya Savina. She was very famous a few years ago."

"She's living in Scotland?"

Alison nodded.

"Somewhere on the Isle of Skye. Kind of a recluse according to the article, which happens to be a reprint. The magazine sent a photographer for photos of her in her retirement, but she chased him off. Without her knowing, he took some shots with a telephoto lens."

"I know how she felt!" sighed Eric. Then he brightened.

"I get it now," he said. "She chased off this guy, but you want to go to Scotland because you figure that you could get an interview with her—as well as a very original paper for the Lit. class."

"Sure," said Alison, "why not? That photographer was probably some dopey *paparazzi* setting his flash off in her face and trying to dig up some scandal about her famous romances. But not us! We'll do enough homework to ask the right questions. About important stuff like her father. And Tolstoy—"

It made sense of a sort to him. Literature and history were favorite subjects for both of them. And photo-journalism was his sister's other big interest. She had saved up and bought a good used Nikon F2, and had carried it along with her on all the campaign stops. She even managed to sell a couple of prints of their grandfather to the Associated Press Wirephoto service.

"I'll admit it sounds like a good thing for you,

Alison, but I'm not sure there's enough in it for me. Besides boning up on the student image, that is," Eric said, dropping back into his earlier listlessness.

Alison was digging in the clutter again with renewed purpose.

"Not another magazine article, please!" Eric begged. "These chance discoveries of yours are beginning to strain your credibility!"

"No—" came the answer. "This time it's a book about the stone carvings—and castles of Scotland. You know you have always dreamed about rescuing a beautiful Scottish lassie from one of those towers."

It was an exaggeration, but it worked. Eric suddenly came alive.

"What do you think?" she said. "We could probably get Dad to okay it—if we went over there together."

"Maybe."

Their father certainly would add that condition to it. He knew the two of them would keep an eye out for each other.

"We'd have to wire him in Kuala Lumpur," Alison chattered on. Dr. Thorne was on leave of absence from Midwest University in Ivy while working as a consultant for the International Agricultural Foundation.

"Come on, Eric. Dad and Gramps owe us one, after all that work we did on the campaign—" Alison raised the back of her hand to her forehead in mock melodrama "—so we can recover from fatigue." She grinned at him. "Well, what do you think?"

"Give me a little more time," said Eric. "And

you'll have to agree that you won't fuss if I take off now and then if it gets boring."

"Wow—I'm going to be late for my photo lab class." Alison jumped off the bed and grabbed her canvas bag by its straps. "Let me know what you decide when I come back, okay?"

After she sprinted from the room, picking up her Secret Service men in her wake, Eric poked through the books spread out on her bed. Most of them were about Scotland, descriptions of the castles and countryside or historical accounts.

Something about the stone carvings, their inscriptions and designs, intrigued him. And the castles—in front of each of them he imagined beautiful Scottish girls with inviting smiles and loaded picnic baskets.

Better yet, there were no celebrity hounds or reporters or Secret Service men within miles.

2 • *Strange Coincidence*

The wind rippling the harbor's slate-gray water was chill enough to drive Alison's gloved hands deeper into the pockets of her down parka. She leaned back against the rail of the ferry and watched the cars being driven across the ramp and on board for the short voyage from the mainland village of Mallaig to Armadale on the Isle of Skye.

Most of the other passengers were inside the enclosed sections of the ferry, warming their faces over steaming paper cups of tea. Eric was beside her, his elbows on the rail and his eyes idly following the gulls as they wheeled and turned above the fishing boats bobbing on the tide. The stony set of his face told Alison that her twin brother's thoughts were absorbed again in the ironic introspection that had hounded him during the final weeks of the election campaign.

"Hey," she said as she playfully nudged him with the

35

toe of one of her deep-lugged hiking boots. "I'll bet anything the Scottish Tourist Board is glad that Bonnie Prince Charlie hid out on the Isle of Skye back in 1745, or whenever it was. What if he'd gone to Muck, or Eigg. Can you imagine anybody making up songs about the 'lovely Muck boat'?"

Eric worked hard to answer with a weak smile. That was about as much as he'd done all the way on the train ride up to Mallaig.

Gamely, she tried again. "You know where the name 'Skye' comes from? Sgiath—an old Celtic word that means 'wing.' From the air the island looks something like a wing—"

"Oh?" Eric lamely feigned interest.

"—so the ancient Celts named it that. It seems a little fishy to me, though. After all, how did the ancient Celts know what the island looked like from the air?"

"Yeah. How did they know that?"

"Do you think it supports the theory that outer space people visited earth a long time ago?" Alison continued. "I can just imagine a bunch of Celts sitting around when a UFO swoops down and a voice says, 'Did you guys know that this place is shaped like a wing?' "

Not even a grunt came from Eric this time. He continued staring out at the harbor, hands clasped in front of him.

"I give up," moaned Alison. Jokes were not her style anyway. She'd just been trying to repay Eric for the times he had clowned her out of the blues.

She knew what was troubling Eric. On the long plane flight over from the States he'd opened up and told her about what he was hoping to find for himself on the trip. Of course she'd known during the last weeks of their grandfather's election campaign that Eric's sudden celebrity status had soured for him. Who wouldn't want to get away from all that?

For that reason, it had been doubly cruel when the very thing that her brother wanted to escape from showed up in Scotland, of all places.

They had checked through customs at Gatwick Airport near London like ordinary young adventurers complete with optimism backpacks and Harvard Student Agency guide books, then caught the train from Kings Cross station all the way through northern England to Scotland. A short ferry ride from the little town of Oban had brought them to the island of Mull, where they had had to leave their bed-and-breakfast lodging at five in the morning to catch the early bus to Fionnphort and the boat to the tiny island of Iona.

Alison had watched the expectant look in her brother's eyes grow sharper with excitement at every stage of their journey. It was the old Eric—alert, excited, interested, fun.

Then it happened.

Alison grimaced as she remembered what had gone on in the cramped little boat before they got to Iona. A group of European tourists alternately stared at Eric and whispered excitedly among themselves.

Once the boat landed, the tourists began their campaign against Eric's privacy in earnest. Cameras clicked as they dogged his steps along the Street of the Dead, a little path of red stones that ran past the graves of the ancient Scottish kings. They ogled him from the pews of the little rough-hewn cathedral and in the small building where the carved flat stones had been stored to save them from the eroding winds.

To the tourists' requests for his autograph, Eric shook his head and dredged up his freshman German.

"Nein, ich kann nicht."

Without Secret Service agents to run interference for them, they had to abandon all hopes of examining the stone carvings.

They escaped on the first boat returning to Mull; then splurged on a taxi to their bed-and-breakfast lodging, just to make sure the tourists didn't hassle them on the bus. The black mood that had settled on Eric after this experience on Iona had stayed with him all the way to Mallaig.

I wish there was something I could do for him, Alison thought. But deep inside she knew that the curious tourists on Iona provided just another incident in a process she had watched with growing anger— anger from not being able to do a single thing about it.

The rattling mechanical noise of the boarding ramps being drawn up broke into her thoughts. All the cars and passengers heading for the Isle of Skye were aboard. The ferry's engines chugged and belched gray steam into the chilly sea air. The gulls flapped away from the boat at the dock, then followed above its churning wake.

Eric pushed himself upright from the rail and stretched the stiff muscles in his arms. He turned to look at Alison and managed a wan smile.

"Brrr," he said. "Think I'll go inside—to get a cup of tea or something. Want one?"

She shook her head.

"Not right now. I kind of like it out here. Besides," she said, as she pulled out her Nikon, "I want to get some shots of the harbor."

"Okay," said Eric. He lifted his pack and headed for the brass-hinged door. "Don't freeze."

Alison leaned over the rail, feeling the ice-cold spray churning up from the wake tingle against her face. On this trip she was expecting to turn a page in her life. This time she would be returning to student life with more than a handful of campaign anecdotes. Now the fascinating information she had gathered on Russian writer Leo Tolstoy propelled her into doing further research here on this adventure to the Isle of Skye. The Tolstoy biography by Henri Troyat that she carried in her pack read like a novel itself. There was something exciting about discovering a link with the past and sharing it with the present.

In the pleasure of running her quest through her mind, she momentarily forgot about her brother. *Maybe,* she thought, as she gazed across the gray waters through which the ferry was cutting, *maybe he'll find something to capture his interest here, too.* She turned that thought into a prayer before she gave herself again to the novelty of her surroundings.

It was a long hike for an old man.

He had parked the rented Morris Minor far below at the edge of the narrow road—no more than an asphalt-paved cow trail really, like a lot of roads on Skye. During the uphill climb, a chilling wind from off the ocean made him pull up the collar of his gray Harris tweed coat to shield his throat. The tendons beneath the pale skin grew tight beneath the rigid and expressionless face.

To an observer, only the old man's eyes would have seemed alive in that pale face, as they flicked from the hand-drawn map he carried to scan the area for any possible observer.

The gnarled hand with a net of blue veins across the back of it pushed the point of the thin silver-headed cane into the pebbles of the dirt path. The old man used each stabbing thrust as a point of leverage, pulling himself up the steep hill the way a mountain climber would use his short-handled axe. His progress was made even more difficult by the limp that caused one leg to twist and drag behind him. The polished black shoes, now coated with dust, were better suited for the cement sidewalks of a city. Here, their smooth soles slipped and skidded on the loose dirt. Still the old man inched his way up the hill, back bent low as he pressed his weight onto the cane. It was obviously a mission he could not assign to anyone else.

At last he gained the top of the hill where he braced himself, leaning on the cane as the wind buffetted his thin frame like an invisible hammer. A few gray strands of hair escaped from his black homberg, and fell in front of his narrowed eyes.

Carefully, the old man eased from his shoulder the strap of his leather bag. Lowering it to the ground, he knelt down and drew the large zipper back by its leather thong. He reached in and pulled out a pair of Zeiss-Ikon binoculars, their black pebbled surfaces filling his pale hands. Snapping off the lens caps, he brought the binoculars to his eyes and scanned the landscape in front of him.

The hill on which the old man stood was one of the highest eye could see along the Isle of Skye's southern coast. From it one could look across the water to Rhum and Eigg, the small barren islands just off of Skye; or even farther on a mistless day to the coast of the Scottish mainland itself. Across the island could be seen the town of Portree; and to the west, the towering jagged shapes of the Black Cuillins, the steepest and most dangerous mountains in all the British Isles.

The old man looked at none of these. He focused his binoculars and scanned the scene for a long time before he found a small cottage on the floor of the valley, nestled in the purple heather and the scrubby brush turning brown with winter. Built long ago, a few modernizing touches had been added: a shingled roof replaced the original thatch, and a large, picture window, double-glazed against the icy winds, had been set into one of the rough stone walls. A gray tendril of smoke drifted up from the cottage's chimney.

Standing far above, the old man adjusted his binoculars, slowly turning the knurled focusing wheel until the cottage's window was brought into razor-sharpness to his eye. The powerful magnification revealed shelves filled to overflowing with books, a grand piano, and several scattered Oriental rugs still lustrous beneath their years of use and lying on hand-hewn plank floors. Banked coals glowed orange and red in the stone fireplace.

The occupant of the cottage stood by the fire, her graying hair pulled back and tied, showing the strong high bones of her face. Her head was bent as she stood lost in thought or prayer.

The figure on the hill above kept her in the double circles of his powerful binoculars' field of vision. As he did, his face took on a look of sinister satisfaction.

The old man watched for several minutes, then lowered the binoculars. His eyes narrowed, as though to keep the anger clenched in his rigid face from draining out. He snapped on the lens caps and replaced the binoculars in his leather bag. Oddly, his hand appeared to gently stroke some object inside the bag for a few moments.

"Soon," he murmured. "Very soon. But first I have to be sure that she's the only one who knows—that she's the very last. I will not rest until I have destroyed them all." He spoke as if swearing an oath before some creature of the nether world.

Something flashed in the darkness of the leather bag. The old man zipped the bag almost closed, leaving a little opening for air, then stood up.

Far across the water he could see the black speck that was the ferry coming over from the mainland. He slung the bag across his shoulder and started down the hill, one foot turning and scraping in the dust and loose rocks. He didn't want to miss the ferry's return trip to the mainland. Before he would return to wrap up his unfinished business here on the Isle of Skye, he had other matters requiring his attention.

"Oh, no!" Eric breathed into his teacup. *Don't tell me it's going to start all over again. I don't think I can handle more of this nonsense.* From his seat by the window inside the upper-deck lounge he saw a girl—her face partly hidden by the camera she held—aiming her lens straight at him. This time he was angry enough to do something about it.

I don't have to put up with this, Eric thought angrily, slapping the paper cup down and spilling brown dregs of tea on the table before him. His hiking boots were noisy on the lounge's deck as he strode over to confront the girl with the camera.

He stood directly in front of her, so close that he could see his reflection in the shining glass of the camera lens. For some reason, the girl didn't lower the camera, but kept it in front of her face. With his hands propped menacingly on his hips, he glared into it.

"You know," he said forcefully, "you may think it's all right to photograph people without their permission, but I think it's rude. How would you like it if everywhere you went somebody was prying at you, and snapping pictures like you were some kind of public monument? Don't you think you'd get sick and tired of it after a while?"

The girl lowered the camera and gazed at Eric without blinking. After a silent face-off that lasted for a few seconds she said coolly, "I'm sure I don't have the slightest idea of what you're talking about."

The calm, even tone of the girl's reply set Eric back momentarily. It was more of a surprise than a punch in the jaw. Without speaking, he studied the face still regarding him without embarrassment.

She looked to be older than he was, perhaps as much as four or five years. She had the pale porcelain skin that one seemed to find only in the British Isles, the cheeks blushing to a faint rose pink. Her shoulder-length red hair, brushed back from her face, was of the golden Scottish shading rather than the darker Irish color.

"You know," she continued quietly with a soft Scottish brogue, "I'm finding you more rude by the second. Do you often attack strangers like this?"

"Wait a minute," said Eric. "You're the one who started this. I was just minding my own business."

"I started it?" she interrupted him. "What on earth are you talking about?" She glared at him in a combination of amazement and exasperation.

44

"Don't play innocent," snapped Eric. "I was just sitting over there, and you started to take my picture."

"Take your picture?" said the girl. "Why, of all the conceited—why should I want a picture of your silly face? I don't even know who you are!"

"Then why were you aiming your camera at me?"

She looked at him now in total contempt. "It so happens," she said with icy dignity, "that I was photographing the way the sunlight reflected off the clouds out the window where you were sitting. I do a spot of painting now and then, and I wanted to get that sort of lighting effect for a seascape I'm planning. Those kinds of details are important to me—though I imagine you've never noticed anything like that, busy as you must be admiring yourself in the mirror all the time."

Eric glanced back at the window. Beyond it the sun scattered on the choppy waves like gold coins.

"You mean—you don't know who I am?" he asked as he faced her again.

Wearily, she sighed and shook her head.

"No. I don't know who you are. And I don't care who you are, either. All I know is that I've had enough of you, or any other conceited tourist who might be aboard. So good day."

Roughly she pushed past him and headed for the stairwell that led to the lower deck.

"Wait!" Eric called. He ran and caught up with her at the head of the polished wooden steps. The girl stopped and leveled her cool gaze at him, as though studying some sort of bothersome insect.

Something in her calm dismissal had turned Eric completely around. He had gone all the way from wanting to be anonymous to the point where he wanted to do anything at all to prove to this girl that he even existed. "Look," he said, "maybe I owe you an apology. Do you follow American politics?"

"Most people do," she said, shrugging noncommitally. "This was an election year, after all."

"Well," said Eric patiently, "the man who was elected Vice President—"

"Yes. His name's Thorne, I believe."

"That's right," he said, nodding in surprised agreement. "Well, I'm his grandson."

The girl's eyes widened for a split second. Eric felt a little gratified that he had at last made some impression on her.

"You must be *daft*," the girl said moments later. "What do the minor relations of the Vice President of the United States have to do with politics? Next I suppose you'll tell me that the President's house cat has cabinet status!"

"But—you see—I helped campaign for him, and—"

"You mean to tell me," she said, "that people in the USA voted for your grandfather's ticket because of you?" She looked at him in almost total amazement.

"Certainly not," said Eric quickly.

"I should hope not." The girl shook her head, baffled by this facet of American culture.

"Look," she went on, "maybe being the grandson

of the Vice President is a very important position in the States—after all, we've got plenty of people who cling to hereditary titles over here—but I really think you're letting it go to your head. I mean, I don't believe most people outside your country care who is the vice-grandson of the President, or whatever it is you are." Giving him a look that held more pity than anything else, she turned away and headed down the stairs.

Eric stood rooted to the spot. The girl's words had struck him like a pitcher of cold water in the face.

Maybe she's right, he thought. *Maybe I have let all that stuff get inside me, and it's changed me without me even knowing it. And then when someone treats me like an ordinary human being, I don't know how to act.*

"Eric! Hey, Eric!"

He turned and saw Alison moving toward him. Faint concern crossed her face as she looked at him.

"Who was that you were talking to?"

"Oh, just someone I met."

"We should be docking soon," said Alison. She pointed to the windows at the front of the lounge. "Look, that must be Armadale Castle up on the hill."

Eric followed the direction of his sister's outstretched finger, but his mind was still on the girl and what she had said to him.

The old man with the limp had returned in time to watch the ferry from Mallaig come slowly up to the pilings of the Armadale dock. He waited for the few cars and passengers arriving on the Isle of Skye to disembark from the ferry, then paid his fare for the crossing back to the mainland. Dragging his twisted leg, he made his way up the boarding ramp.

Once aboard, he stood near the ramp at the ferry's side rail, waiting for its departure. His eyes, deepset in his seamed face, scanned the few arriving passengers still standing on the dock beside their baggage. The old gentleman appeared to have the type of mind that never tired, but was always watching and noting even the smallest details. He had survived that way.

His eyes rested on two passengers who had just disembarked: a girl wearing a down parka jacket and hiking boots. Her dark hair, pulled back from a lovely face, was tied simply. A backpack rested on the dock beside her. A boy about the same age and with similar facial features joined her. Before the ferry's departure the old man could hear their conversation.

"Hey, Alison, the fellow in the office says it'll be about fifteen minutes before the bus to Broadford gets here." The girl nodded, and the boy headed for the other end of the dock to pick up his backpack.

Unnoticed by the girl, the old man aboard the ferry continued to study her. When her brother rejoined her, their conversation resumed. Because their backs were turned, he couldn't follow it. But he stiffened when he heard some words in their conversation that had been ringing in his own mind for at least a quarter of a century.

48

"Anya Savina . . . notes . . ."

His was not a mind to believe in coincidences. What reason would these two obviously American young people have to see Anya Savina? How had they discovered where she lived? What notes were they hoping to find? What's the connection here?

A decision was forging itself, like a new link on an ice-cold chain. It looked as if there would be more business to take care of when he returned to the Isle of Skye than he had originally counted on.

3 • Introduction to the Fraudulent Stones

By the time Eric came downstairs, Alison was working her way steadily through the crisp rashers of bacon and coddled eggs that Mrs. Morland, the proprietor of the bed-and-breakfast lodging, had set out in the dining room. She was pouring more tea into her cup when she looked up and saw her brother rubbing a last remnant of the night's dreams from his eyes.

"Well, good morning, sleepyhead," said Alison. "I almost didn't leave any for you." Her brown eyes regarded him over the rim of her teacup.

"Mmph," grunted Eric. He was never as alert in the mornings as Alison was. Even as a kid back home in Ivy, Illinois, she had often been out of bed before the sun came up, just to catch the last straggler fireflies in a Mason jar.

"Eat something," Alison said. "You look like the last stages of protein deprivation."

As he filled his plate, Eric glanced out the window. The weather seemed milder than yesterday when they had climbed off the bus in Broadford. From his chair by the window, Eric watched shafts of morning sunlight glistening on the calm waters of Broadford's little bay. The winter was late setting in this year, their hostess told them, but the snow and ice would soon come.

"So!" said Alison, pushing aside her plate. "Are you going to thank me for getting us out of Washington and into this calm and quiet part of the past?"

She pushed back her chair and stood poised for departure. "I'm ready now for our little adventure. What about you?"

"Not really," Eric said, failing to match her enthusiasm. He took a slice of cold toast from the silver rack, marveling again at the British device apparently designed to cool the toast promptly. "Do we really have to start today?"

"Why not?" Alison grinned at him. "Got to track down the elusive Anya Savina."

"Don't you think you should call her on the phone first?" He nibbled on the bacon. At least it was still warm.

"Don't be silly," Alison responded. "She's a recluse, remember? And as any thinking person knows, recluses . . . don't . . . have . . . phones."

"Oh, you already checked the phone directory?" Eric nodded toward the table that held the telephone books in the hallway.

"Well, yes, as a matter of fact I did."

"So much for what any thinking person knows," said Eric dryly.

"You're impossible." Alison grinned, taking her parka off the back of the chair. "Okay, we'll start out tomorrow. Meanwhile, I'm going to poke around the village and find out about transportation. That should give you time to forget those awful tourists. If I'm not back for lunch, I'll see you at dinner."

At her usual speed, she dashed out of the room, snatched up her canvas bag in the hallway, and was out the front door.

"I'm not going to let one of Eric's moods spoil this expedition," she muttered to herself. "Besides, I promised he could cut out when he wanted to. Just my luck that he wants to cut out the first day."

Eric sat at the table, dabbing the corner of his toast into the egg yolk. Like the weather, his mood had lightened from the day before. The brief conversation with the girl aboard the ferry had blown away some of the fog from his mind.

He wished he could see her again, but that didn't seem likely. Even though Skye was an island, it was a big one. You couldn't count on running into somebody as interesting as that every day.

Alison pushed open the glass door of the Scottish Tourist Board office. The kindly lady behind the counter was the same one who had helped them find a vacant pair of bed-and-breakfast rooms the day before.

"Hello, love," she said as Alison entered. "How did you like Mrs. Morland's? You and your brother aren't leaving us so soon, are you?"

"It's wonderful," said Alison. "Great breakfast. And no, we'll be staying a while longer. I just came in to see if I could get some directions."

"Well, that's one thing we've got plenty of." The lady waved at the wall behind Alison. It was covered with wire racks filled with maps and guide books for different areas of Scotland. In the center was a bulletin board crowded with announcements of local happenings, church socials, and *ceilidhs,* the traditional gatherings of Celtic pipe music and songs.

"Where do you want to get to?" she asked.

"The place I'm looking for doesn't seem to be on the maps," Alison answered politely. Politician's granddaughter that she was, she selected several inexpensive souvenirs to help prime the information she was seeking.

"I'm looking for a place called the Tolstoyan Community," she said after her packages were wrapped and paid for.

"That old place?" The woman looked surprised. "It used to be called the Mullington Barakha Community. No, I don't suppose you'd find it on a map. Wherever did you hear about those people?"

"They were mentioned in a magazine article I read," explained Alison. The article about Anya Savina had said that the aged concert pianist had gone to stay with the Tolstoyan Community on the Isle of Skye. Although Anya had later left this group to live alone, they were still Alison's only source for learning Anya Savina's current whereabouts.

"Frankly," said the lady behind the counter, "I'm not even sure how many of those religious folk are still alive."

Alison's heart sank a little with the woman's words.

"And there's really no easy way to get out there to see," she went on. "You'd have to catch the postal bus and ride out with the mail carrier. It's at the end of his route, though, so you wouldn't get there until late in the afternoon, and then it would still be quite a long hike to get to the community itself."

"Oh." The trek sounded a little intimidating to Alison. "There's no other way to get there?"

The woman pondered, scratching her forehead with the corner of her glasses.

"Well, somebody from there usually comes into town on Monday mornings to pick up supplies. Perhaps you could get a lift with him, if you can catch him." She leaned across the counter in order to peer out the window at the store across the street.

"Ah, you're in luck, lass! There he is right now!"

The woman scooted around the corner of the counter and out the door of the shop.

"Mr. Nevis," she called, waving her hand. "Could you step over here for a bit?"

Alison peered around her to see. In front of the little store a man was bent over, loading a cardboard box of supplies into the trunk of an aging Austin sedan. The man looked up and smiled. Alison wasn't sure what a 20th-century Tolstoyan would look like, but this one seemed jarringly out of character. He slammed the trunk lid shut and ambled across the street toward them.

"Good morning!" He smiled at Alison. "I'm Brother Nevis."

"Mr. Nevis," said the woman, ignoring the prefix of brotherhood, "this young lady would like to get out to the Tolstoyan place. Could she hop a ride with you?"

The man shrugged as he slid his hands into the pockets of his faded smock.

"I don't see why not," he said, eyeing Alison critically. The smock, patched in several places, topped a pair of antique woolen trousers. In Alison's view, he looked more like a hunter or fisherman than a member of a religious sect.

"Come on, then," he said, starting across the street to his car. "Best get started. It's a little way to go."

Was Alison imagining it, or did he seem a little annoyed by this out-of-season tourist's interest in the Tolstoyan settlement?

"Oh, but I don't want to go today, Mr.—Brother—Nevis. I was just inquiring about arrangements to get out there. I want to go tomorrow. There are two of us—my brother and me. I understand we can get a ride back with the mail carrier."

"I didn't catch the name," the man said.

"Alison," the Thorne twin answered, hesitant for

some unexplained reason to add her family name.

The Tolstoyan seemed instantly aware of the omission.

"My brother and I are staying at Mrs. Morland's bed-and-breakfast—" Alison filled in the silence.

"Well, if you're here at the same time tomorrow morning, I'll give you a lift," he called over his shoulder as he turned and walked away. The door of his aging sedan squealed in protest as he opened it. He revved the motor and made a hurried U-turn in the almost deserted main street.

"That's odd," the shopkeeper observed. "He's heading in the opposite direction. And he said he'd be back tomorrow. I've never known him to be in town more than once a fortnight."

Alison headed for the post office to mail cards to Gram and Gramps in Washington, to Dad in Kuala Lumpur, and to Aunt Rose back home in Ivy, Illinois. She was pleased with the arrangements she had made for tomorrow. As she was leaving the post office, the ancient Austin passed her again heading back through the town. The driver seemed too preoccupied to notice her.

She bought a packet of fish and chips, and ate them down at the pier. Then she headed back to Mrs. Morland's, intending to read more chapters of the fascinating Tolstoy biography. The more she knew about Tolstoy and his writings, she figured, the better her chance of getting to Anya Savina.

She was still puzzling over the relationship of Brother

Nevis to the group when she turned into Mrs. Morland's rambling establishment.

"I'm not sure I like that man," she told herself as she climbed the stairs to her room.

Revived by his ample breakfast, Eric sauntered down the main street of Broadford. There was little to see or do except enjoy the peace and quiet, and breathe deep the sea breeze coming in from the harbor nearby. This suited Eric perfectly. For the moment he was content to walk with the sun warm across his shoulders, with no plan on his mind other than to watch the waves lapping the rocks. The tourist season was long since past in this tiny outlying region. It was a good place to be anonymous again.

"Eric! Eric Thorne!" An unfamiliar voice from behind him broke the still country air like a stone through a pane of glass.

He spun around, experiencing once more the mixture of anger and dismay that attended hearing his own name on the lips of some stranger. His reaction was replaced by amazement when he saw who it was. Running toward him along the unpaved path beside the road was the girl from the ferry. Her red hair flashed as flamelike in the sun as her temper had the day before.

"I'm terribly sorry," she gasped as she caught up with him, panting to catch her breath. "I wanted to apologize for the way I acted yesterday. I hope you'll forgive me. There was no reason to be so rude."

"Well, thanks," said Eric with obvious surprise. "I mean, you really don't have to feel that way. I was the one who was out of line. I shouldn't have come storming up at you the way I did, shouting my silly head off."

The girl smiled at him. "Oh, but I think I understand now why you acted that way, Mr. Thorne—"

"Eric," he broke in. "Call me Eric."

Her smile grew wider. "All right," she said. "And I'm Katherine. Katherine MacLeod." She extended her hand gravely. "Call me Katy—most people do."

"It's a pleasure," he said, shaking her hand. "I didn't expect to see you again, Katy."

A slight blush rose beneath her fair skin.

"I wouldn't have thought you'd ever want to," she said. "Not after yesterday. Terribly uncalled for behavior, I'm afraid. After all, you at least had some justification for the way you acted."

"How do you mean?" he asked, estimating the girl's age to be at least twenty.

Katy walked slowly along the path with him. "Oh, I think I deduced a few things about you, Eric. I imagine I might feel pretty much the same way you do, and act the same way, if I were in your place."

"Oh? How did you find out about all that?"

"After I got off the ferry from Mallaig," she said, "I took the bus to Portree, further north here on Skye. There's a well-stocked library there. I went digging through the back issues of some American news weeklies, just to see if what you had said about being the

58

grandson of the Vice President was true or not. I wanted to know whether you were bragging or crazy when you came flying at me aboard the ferry.''

"And you found out I was crazy,'' said Eric with a grin.

"No,'' she replied, "but judging from some accounts of your experiences in California, they must have hounded you almost to death!'' Eric was grateful for her understanding.

"I really felt quite sorry for you. And then to come all the way to the Isle of Skye and find another pesky photographer aiming at you—well, it's quite under-standable why you blew up the way you did.''

"I've probably become a bit paranoid about it all.'' Eric couldn't believe his luck at finding her again as he picked up the conversation. "Though I suppose I should learn a lesson from this. I really shouldn't judge everybody I come across on the basis of the worst ones I've seen.''

"Oh, we all do that sometimes. It's just part of human nature, I suppose. That's why I wanted to find you and apologize.''

"How did you find me, anyway?'' asked Eric.

"It wasn't hard,'' she said. "You weren't on the bus from Armadale to Portree, so I assumed you had taken the later one here to Broadford. I asked around, and the lady at the Tourist Office told me you were here. Then it was just a matter of keeping my eyes open. After all, it's a pretty small town—it would be hard for anyone to stay hidden very long, even a notorious camera-shy recluse like yourself." She smiled at him as she added the last words.

The path curved toward the harbor, and Eric could hear the low waves swishing the rocks along the shore.

"Well, I'm glad you did find me," he said, returning her friendly smile. "Not that I wanted an apology or anything. I guess mainly I just wanted to talk to someone like you."

They walked without speaking for a while, enjoying the sounds of the birds and the surf. Eric broke the silence.

"What are your plans for the rest of the morning?"

"I've arranged to rent a car from a shopkeeper and drive out to photograph the local standing rock collection," Katherine replied. "My aunt who lives near here told me about it. It puzzles me why it isn't mentioned in the tourist guides."

Eric's interest was stirred immediately.

"Mind if I tag along?" he asked. Her quick agreement brought the old sparkle to his eyes.

An hour later the tiny Morris Minor Katy had rented pulled up beside a weathered gate. A metal mailbox had the words TOLSTOYAN COMMUNITY painted on it.

"What a super coincidence!" Eric called out. "My sister and I plan to come here tomorrow."

The arch over the gate had some words Katherine recognized as Arabic.

"That's odd," said Eric, "I thought they would be Russian."

The path sloped up the hill, curving across the flank in a gradual ascent. At the crest of the hill they stopped to gain their bearings. Behind them was the road at the hill's base, and on the other side of it, a much higher range of hills overlooking the one they stood upon. Jagged tumbles of gray boulders, the debris cast aside by ancient glaciers, crowned the steep hills.

In front of them, the path branched in two. The left fork curved down into a low valley, at the bottom of which a group of low half-timbered buildings were clustered. Gardens, which stretched beyond the houses, and several rows of greenhouses, glass panes glinting in the sunlight, completed the scene. A trail of smoke rising from the chimney of one of the buildings was the only evidence that the buildings were currently inhabited.

"That must be your Tolstoyan place," Katherine pointed. "We want the trail to the right."

It led to a small level section of ground, ringed by the skeletal remains of a few dead and blackened trees. What filled the center of the space was a group of enormous stones, some twelve to fifteen feet high and roughly rectangular in shape, each with one end buried in the ground so that they stood upright like a loose formation of granite sentries.

Eric's first thought upon seeing the stones was of Stonehenge or Avebury "standing stone" arrangements.

"This place resembles an open-air temple or ritual site," Katy offered.

"Or maybe a celestial observatory corresponding to various stars in the sky," Eric suggested.

As they debated the various possibilities, Eric realized his lovely companion was more delightful by the minute. The wealth of information she was pouring out was impressive. He did feel a tug of guilt for telling Alison he wasn't interested in trekking around, and then ending up at the very place she wanted to see.

As he followed Katy toward the unusual rough-hewn stone shapes, they stopped at the sound of a voice from among the stones. It was a woman's voice raised in anger, punctuated by the sharp *thwack* of one object hitting another.

"Disgraceful!" the voice was saying as they came close enough to make out the words. "Absolutely disgraceful!"

Middle-aged but with a vigorously youthful stride, a woman was pacing from one stone to another. Improbable as it seemed, she was cursing them roundly, and every once in a while lifting her stout hiking staff to strike one of the stones a solid blow—as if it were possible to chastise them for whatever fault it was she found in them.

She was dressed in a heavy tweed coat of mannish cut, topping a skirt of the same fabric, her legs clad in heavy gray wool stockings and a sturdy pair of cleated walking shoes. A white pith helmet, straight from some African safari gone astray, made her appearance even more bizarre. A pair of field glasses hanging from a strap around her neck bounced against

her as she strode angrily among the stones.

"The effrontery of it!" she exclaimed, standing before another one. "Shocking!" *Thwack* went the hiking staff again on the unfeeling stone.

Watching her, neither Katy nor Eric tried to hide their amusement.

The woman heard their laughter and spotted them at the head of the dirt path. Instead of being embarrassed at being caught in her odd behavior, the woman nodded her head as if she were agreeing with them.

"You're absolutely right, my dears," she said forthrightly. "These stones are quite ridiculous."

For a giddy moment, Eric felt as if he had blundered into an Alice-in-Wonderland world. He had never expected to find himself in Scotland asking about the merits of enormous stones from a slightly looney, tweedy lady.

"Whatever's wrong with them?" he baited. "They look perfectly fine to me."

"You must be joking," the woman admonished him. "These stones are frauds! Palpable frauds! Stuck here in the ground with no regard for historical accuracy at all!" She flipped a scornful hand at the nearest one to her. "Just look at the big silly thing. Frankly, I find it embarrassing—you'd expect the good English gentleman of the Victorian era who put them here to have done better than this shoddy pile."

"Keep her talking, Eric," Katherine whispered in Eric's ear. "She's a better photographic study than the stones themselves."

"You mean—they're not real?" asked Eric. He stepped inside the circle and gazed up at the towering shapes. "I mean, not that they're not real stones, but they weren't put here by the ancient pagans?"

"Surely, young man, you didn't think so. Why, of course they weren't! A respectable Druid wouldn't be caught dead in a place like this."

"Then who did put them here?" asked Eric. The woman's brisk manner of speaking had propelled her into a full-fledged conversation without regard for introductions.

"Oh, it was that silly Thomas Mullington," said the woman. "The same one that founded the first hodge-podge religious community here. They call it something else now." She jabbed with her walking stick in the direction of the valley and its buildings.

"When was that?" Eric asked, hoping to get some information to take back to Alison.

"Sometime around the turn of the century, he erected this stage-play Stonehenge. What could he have been thinking of? And to do such a poor job of it, too." She tsked-tsked softly to herself, shaking her head at the stupidity of the stones' long-dead designer.

"They look very impressive to me," said Eric. The stones were such obvious underdogs against the woman's barrage of criticism that he felt like defending them.

"My dear," continued the woman, "they're all wrong. They're not even the right kind of stone. This is just some local rock quarried here on the Isle of

Skye, not like the authentic stones at Avebury and else-where. And look at these chiseled inscriptions on them. These marks are just gibberish!"

She glared at the nearest offending stone as if contemplating some way to give it an even sounder thrashing than she already had.

"You sound as if you know a great deal about these kind of stones," Katy said diplomatically, coming forward for a close-up.

The woman scrabbled through the contents of her deep coat pockets and drew out a rumpled-looking pamphlet.

"Here, take this—you'll find it educational, I'm sure."

Eric took the pamphlet and read the cover. BRITAIN'S STONE CIRCLES—RITUAL SITES OR ASTRONOMIC PRECURSORS? The title ran above a line drawing of Stonehenge. Below that were the words *By Dr. Hermione Rockingham, LL.D., President, Anglo-Celtic Antiquities Research Society.*

"Thank you," he said, tucking the pamphlet into his pocket.

"Have you been to Avebury yet?" The imposing woman asked.

"No," Eric said. "Not yet."

"Ah, now that's a truly fine stone circle. Most people go to see Stonehenge, but I prefer Avebury myself. It's a pity what happened to some of the stones there didn't happen to these frauds."

"What happened to them?"

"Oh, some of the early Christian villagers who lived near the Avebury circle apparently decided that the stones were relics of an ancient pagan religion and should be destroyed, so they set about the job of doing just that. Their method was to dig a large pit beside one of the stones, fill the pit with straw, then topple the stone over into the pit. They then would set fire to the straw under the stone. When the stone was hot, the villagers would pour cold water onto it, and the stone would crack into pieces small enough to be broken up by hammers. They got rid of quite a few of the stones that way; there are little concrete pylons there now to mark the spaces where the missing stones probably stood. I suppose they would have destroyed all the stones if an accident hadn't interrupted their work."

"An accident?" echoed Eric. "What kind of accident?"

"A rather amusing one, in a morbid sort of way," said Dr. Rockingham. "The villagers were just finishing the pit for one of the stones and one man was still in it. Of its own accord, the stone toppled into the pit, crushing him. The villagers must have decided that the devil was still in the stones, and it would be the wisest course not to fool with them any further. I can just imagine them all running for the safety of the village church. Sometime in the eighteenth century, the fatal stone was dug up, and the skeleton of the poor fellow was still under it, complete to the coins that had been in his pocket. It's all in there," she said, pointing to the pamphlet protruding from Eric's jacket.

Eric smiled, amused at the woman's sympathy for the ancient monument. His own sympathies leaned toward the Christian villagers.

Eric felt a gentle tug on his arm and turned to see Katy pointing to her watch. Obviously she wanted to terminate the lecture.

"Thanks for the information," Eric said politely to Dr. Rockingham. "It is very interesting."

"Yes, of course," the woman answered, obviously cheered that she had exposed the fake stones to at least two members of the next generation. "Do try to get down to Avebury instead of wasting your time here."

As they turned away, they saw the formidable woman give one of the stones a parting blow before striding off.

Still laughing about the odd encounter, Eric and Katy stopped at a small tea shop near the tourist office.

"You two may be my last customers for the season," the rosy-cheeked shopkeeper said when she brought their order. There were corners of condensation framing the tiny panes of the shop window overlooking the sea. Baking smells drifted from the ovens in the rear.

"What a super ending for a surprise day!" Eric said, looking into a pair of widely spaced blue eyes. They twinkled back at him as their owner tasted a fresh baked scone. Eric followed suit, thinking how much he liked older—and Scottish—girls. No wonder so many songs were written about them.

"The last ferry leaves in thirty minutes," she announced, all too soon. "It looks like rain out there. I should like to make it before it starts pouring."

Eric followed Katy's gaze to the brooding, dark-edged storm clouds swelling just above the ocean. Again he felt a twinge about cutting out on Alison and going to the Tolstoyan place without her. He hoped she wouldn't be caught in foul weather as she went poking about the island on her own.

"I'd like you to meet my sister," he told Katherine as she picked up her things. "Are you sure you must leave today?"

"I wish I could stay longer, Eric," the girl answered shaking her head. "But I really must get back to Edinburgh and be ready to pick up my classes again at the University."

Eric's heart sank a little.

"I'll write you sometime," she promised quickly. "Here, write your address on a corner of this."

Eric tore a bit of paper from the piece she handed him and scribbled down his home address in Ivy. Then he gave the torn piece to Katherine and absentmindedly slipped the folded paper into his own pocket.

"I hope your Tolstoy project works out for you and your sister," the Scottish girl said as they parted. "I think you may enjoy more than you know becoming a serious student again." Her voice grew more personal. "I also hope you find a way to deal with your new public image, Eric."

"Being with you today has helped a lot," he

answered earnestly. "At least you believe I don't enjoy getting special attention for nothing but an accident of birth!"

Eric watched the figure against the rail of the ferry until it was a speck on the horizon. He walked slowly through the little town, happier than he had been for a long time, and eager to share his day with Alison.

He was too preoccupied to notice a lone figure sitting in an ancient Austin across the street from Mrs. Morland's inn.

4 • Abrupt Dismissal

The man who called himself Brother Nevis was folding a gray army blanket over the protruding springs on the front seat of the Austin when Eric and Alison arrived in front of the Tourist Board Office next morning. He motioned Alison to sit beside him, and Eric crawled in the back.

They started off with a clash of gears, and soon the little road from Broadford was running deep into the brown hills of Skye.

"So tell me," said Brother Nevis, "why do you want to visit the Tolstoyan Community? Don't tell me that old biddy at the tourist office led you to believe it is one of the sights to see around here."

Alison gazed out the side window at the purple and brown clusters of heather. "No. We've got our own reasons for going out there."

"Oh? And what might they be?" A tone of con-

71

trolled curiosity sounded in the questioner's voice.

"We're looking for someone. Someone we have reason to believe that the people at the Community might be able to help us find."

The driver let the conversation drop, whistling a cheery scrap of a Highlands reel through his teeth as he drove.

They questioned him about the passing sights as they rattled along. Eric thought he answered them amazingly well for the relative newcomer to the community he claimed to be. He also seemed to be rather expert at steering the conversation away from reference to Tolstoy or the Community whenever that subject came up. He preferred to ask questions, especially about the political system in the United States and members of the government.

"Here it is," he said finally, braking the car to a stop at the side of the road.

"The main entrance is just a little way up the path there. Motor vehicles are not allowed on the grounds. You'll have to enter on foot. I hope you don't mind a bit of a walk. We wouldn't want to interrupt the meditations with this noisy Austin."

"Oh, we don't mind walking," said Eric. "In fact, I know the way. I was out here yesterday."

Alison was examining the simple wooden gate with its unpainted arch, and the ramshackle fence almost overgrown with weeds. She turned up her nose a little at Eric's remark. It wasn't fun being scooped. After all, she had planned this venture in the first place. But she was glad that her brother was in a congenial mood.

"Well, I hope you find what you're looking for," said Trevor Nevis. "The postal bus goes by here about three in the afternoon. You can ride back with him to Broadford. Just stand here and flag him down."

"How much do we owe you?" Eric asked, reaching for his wallet.

"Nary a penny," was the good-natured reply.

"It was really very kind of you," Alison put in.

"No trouble at all."

With a wave and a rattle of gears the Austin prepared for a takeoff. The car moved about twenty feet, then suddenly there was a squeal of brakes. Eric and Alison waited as the ancient machine reversed toward them.

"I might as well tell you, since you'll find out soon enough—I'm not a member of the Community," Nevis shouted to them from the driver's seat. "I rent a small cottage from them on the edge of their grounds and work out the payment by doing errands. Neither the Tolstoyans nor I want to get involved with the town, so the arrangement suits me just fine."

"But the lady in the tourist shop thinks you're a member. Perhaps the whole village does too," Alison put in.

"That suits me fine too, Miss. I can come and go freely without having to make small talk and answer a lot of questions."

"Aren't you afraid we'll blow your cover?" Eric asked.

Nevis smiled, but said no more. Soon car and driver were in motion again, building up speed as they disappeared into the hills.

"I knew all the time he couldn't possibly be a Tolstoyan," Alison commented archly as they turned away from the road and climbed the hill.

There the path to the Mullington Barakha Community's buildings sloped gently beneath their hiking boots. A startled red chicken flapped out of the brush by the side of the path, and scurried ahead of them to the safety of a ramshackle hen house beside one of the buildings. The impression was that of a once bustling farm that had now lapsed into easy retirement. As they approached the settlement, it was decided Alison would do the talking.

Standing at the nearest building's front door, they observed that the same Arabic symbols that had been carved over the gate at the roadside were also incised above the doorway. There was no door buzzer or knocker, but a large copper bell, green with age, hanging beside the post. Eric gave the bell's rope a few tugs and its sharp clatter broke through the valley's quiet.

But the only answer was a squawk or two, the muttered clucking of the hens in their coop. The twins waited a few moments and were about to ring the bell again when they heard footsteps behind them.

"Oh, there's no need for you to do that," a voice said quietly. "I perceived you coming down the footpath."

They turned to see the man who had spoken to them standing off a few yards away. Here, at last was someone who looked like a disciple of the Russian author, Alison thought. A shock of snow-white hair crowned his head in an unruly, Einstein-like halo. His face, lined by years and tanned to a brown leather like that of a desert nomad, broke into a warm smile. He wore a simple white cotton cassock and dark trousers soiled with small agricultural chores. His clothing hung loosely on his thin, straight frame.

"I hope we're not interrupting your work or anything," said Alison as she stepped away from the building's door.

"Not at all," the man said. "Frankly, I was hiding." He tapped beside his eyes with one lean brown forefinger. "I'm afraid these aren't quite so sharp for details at long distances anymore. When I saw you round the curve, I thought it might be our visitor of yesterday returning, in which case I felt that absenting myself might be the most prudent course to follow.

"You mean Dr. Rockingham?" asked Eric.

"Yes, that's right." The man nodded. "That Rockingham person seriously disturbed the peace around here yesterday. Do you know the woman?"

"I know she certainly has forceful opinions," Eric offered. "I only met her yesterday myself, quite by chance."

"Well, she and her forceful opinions exploded all over the landscape like a Mills grenade. I feel as though I should be picking shrapnel out of myself still." His smile grew wider, showing a line of brilliant white teeth.

"But enough of that. You're obviously not representing Dr. Rockingham."

"My name's Alison—Alison Thorne, and this is my brother, Eric."

"I'm very pleased to meet you." He gave a slight bow. "I'm Brother Thomas."

"Would you be any relation to the Thomas Mullington Dr. Rockingham spoke about?" Eric was quick to ask.

"Oh, she must have been referring to my great uncle, the one who founded the community here. I was named after him, although I do not follow his views. I hope her comments didn't set your mind against my illustrious ancestor?"

"Come to think of it, she seemed to have a low opinion of him," admitted Eric.

"Many people thought ill of him when he was alive, and still do now that he's long dead," said Brother Thomas. "For example, that group of standing stones that our good Dr. Rockingham despises so much." He lifted his hand and pointed to where the stones were hidden by the rise of the hill. "She sees it as just a mockery of the type of stones found here in the British Isles—thus she shows her limited perception. My great uncle actually modeled them after certain stone figures and temple carvings he encountered during his years of wandering in Central Asia.

"But that was many years ago. I came back to the old place about twenty years ago, and saw it as an ideal spot for pursuing my own religious beliefs, which are modeled after the teachings of Leo Tolstoy.

"Enough of that. Now, tell me, what brings you two here?"

"We want to find Anya Savina," said Alison.

"You know she is no longer with us?" Brother Thomas asked, giving Alison a penetrating look.

"Yes," she replied, "but we hoped you would help us find her."

The old man appeared to ignore the request.

"I'm afraid the Tolstoyan Community's active life is pretty much at an end," he continued. "Come along, and I'll show you the grounds." He led them away from the buildings toward a rustic arbor.

"As late as fifteen years ago, we had over fifty students here year-round, studying Tolstoy's writings and listening to my lectures and to a select group of other teachers. Some of Russia's greatest writers taught here in the early years, but that was quite a long time ago.

"I found the business of administering both the school and the farm a bit taxing. Gradually, I cut back on the Community's activities, and gave my blessing to some of the younger disciples. There's quite a large school in London now, and a couple in California.

"Here, there are only five brothers left, including myself. We just run a small printing press now to publish articles written by the members. I was running the press myself until quite unexpectedly a young man came and offered his assistance. He's been doing the heavy stuff—running the press and binding the copies—ever since. That frees me for the more scholarly part." At that moment they were passing a small building from which came a rhythmic thumping noise of machinery. Brother Thomas rapped on one of its small windows.

"Alfred! Show yourself for a moment, and say hello to Alison and Eric Thorne."

A young man's face bobbed up in the window for a moment. He smiled shyly, then said, "Hello. I hope you'll excuse me, but the ink feed on the press is acting up a bit." He disappeared once more.

"Sort of a monastic life for a young man," said Brother Thomas as they walked away from the print shop. "But no doubt he earns a measure of spiritual merit from his work."

Brother Thomas led them to a plain wooden bench beneath a tree shorn of its leaves by the advancing winter. "Come and sit down," he said. "Now tell me again why you've come here." His gentle smile played again on his face. "If you've come seeking spiritual enlightenment . . ."

"Not exactly," said Alison, sitting down on the bench beside the old man. "Our faith in God and in Jesus Christ means much to us, and we believe in the Bible."

"So you're Christians?" interrupted Mullington.

Both Alison and Eric nodded quickly in assent.

"Good! Too many people your age go looking for cheap baubles and substitutes from exotic lands."

"We're here looking for someone rather than something," Alison went on. "We were hoping you could tell us where we could find Anya Savina."

The Tolstoyan's eyes tensed with caution for a split second.

"Why are you seeking Anya? Whatever do you know about her?"

"You do know where she lives, don't you? We have come a long way to find her."

Brother Thomas gazed off into the distance, stroking his chin in thought.

"My children," he said at last, measuring his words, "Anya Savina is someone who has earned her privacy, and privacy is more important to her now than ever." The old man paused as though overcome by some ominous reminder. "If I were to direct you to her, I'd have to know that your desire to talk with her is a worthy one." His thoughtful, deep-set eyes rested on Alison as if to see down into her soul.

Alison hesitated and Eric encouraged her to go on. Their reason for wanting to see the aged pianist was not easy to express to an absolute stranger.

But the look in Eric's eyes assured Alison that he trusted this gentle old man. He looked as if he guarded secrets and mysterious quests of his own.

"All right," said Alison, "I'll tell you why we want to see Anya Savina."

There was no going back now. Brother Thomas had as much as hinted that Anya's safety depended on her privacy. Only the simple truth about their reasons for seeking her would satisfy this man.

"I guess you know we're Americans?" Alison began.

The Tolstoyan nodded pleasantly.

"Our grandfather, E. Bradford Thorne, was running on Joseph Andrews' ticket as Vice President."

There was no surprise or unusual interest on the face of Brother Thomas at this announcement. He motioned for her to continue.

"Eric and I received permission from our high school to be absent from our classes and join Gramps in the presidential campaign. At one point Eric became a special target of the media, and some untrue things were printed about him.

"When it was all over and our grandfather was elected," Alison continued, "we felt uncomfortable about going back home and being treated like celebrities—as if we were somebody special just because of Gramps. We wanted to do something to help us feel we were still just normal American teenagers, and that all that publicity hadn't changed us."

"Besides, we needed to do something to ease us back into the routine of being students again after all the excitement of the campaign," Eric added.

"Well," Alison went on, encouraged by the kindly look in the old man's eyes, "I got in touch with our school to find out what subjects we were going to study next semester, hoping to find one in which we could do some interesting work on our own. Tolstoy's *War and Peace* and *Anna Karenina* were on the reading list for study in our literature class.

"I just happened to notice an interview with a Russian concert pianist in a magazine, almost that same week. It was kind of interesting to me because I am studying piano myself."

"Go on," Brother Thomas urged politely.

"The pianist was Anya Savina. During the interview, she mentioned that her father actually *knew* Tolstoy, and that she had some letters the author wrote to her father, discussing his work on the very books we were going to study. I think they were written from a place called Yasnaya Polyana—"

"Yes, yes—that was his home about 130 miles from Moscow. I know of those letters, of course." Brother Thomas interjected.

"So that's why we're here—to ask the lady if it would be possible for her to read the letters to us and talk to us about her father's relationship with Leo Tolstoy."

Then she added, "Eric here is probably more interested in stone carvings and in Scottish history."

"Oh, but I'm ready to explore the Tolstoy material, too," Eric added quickly to assure Brother Thomas of his genuine interest in meeting Anya Savina.

"Of course, we won't deny we were excited about coming to Scotland. But our main reason was to do some research before going back to our classroom studies," Alison explained.

Alison paused, realizing that the Tolstoyan's expression had suddenly changed.

"Did the article, by any chance, mention the name of her father?" he asked.

"Yes, his name was Valentin Sovorin, but that's all she would say about him." she said.

Brother Thomas jumped from the weathered bench, obviously in great distress.

"You mean that name was printed in the article you read?"

Alison nodded, surprised at the reaction. The man in the white cassock paced back and forth in visible agitation, forgetting that they were present.

"I cannot explain my reaction to what you have just said," he said after a long time. "Rest assured it does not concern you. I will direct you to Anya's cottage not far from here. But you must tell her all you have told me. I cannot vouch for what her answer will be."

He pointed back over the hills to where the road lay, then gave them a few simple directions for finding the path that led to Anya Savina's cottage.

"Thanks so much," said Alison, lifting her bag to her shoulder.

"You've been very helpful." Eric echoed her words.

"I wish you God's blessing on your quest," said brother Thomas, inclining his head.

They saw the old gentleman watching them as they walked. *Why did he seem so troubled over the information they had just given him?* they wondered.

Within less than a mile, they came to the narrow break in the scrubby hedge that ran next to the path, just as Brother Thomas had described it. It was well hidden, and would have been easy enough to overlook if they hadn't been clued in on it. When they had pushed their way past the stiff branches of the hedge, they found a small trail that looked like it was made by wild animals running on their secret errands. A few trodden-down places in the heather had sunk into a bog of mud from the last rains. As they walked, their deep-lugged hiking boots left their prints like teeth marks in the damp ground.

Lying at the bottom of a valley with inclines steeper than the site of the Tolstoyan Community, was the little cottage, just as the old man had promised. Alison recognized the cottage from the pictures in the magazine. It had a shingled roof, rough stone walls— a picture window was set into one of them—even the thread of gray smoke curling from the chimney.

"We're here, Eric! Can you believe it?" Alison's heart beat a little faster with the excitement of her quest. Careful not to slip on the sharp incline that the path took down into the valley, they hurried toward the cottage.

But when they reached the cottage door, they both hesitated. Here again, a few strokes of Arabic lettering were carefully painted on the knotted wood.

"Do you suppose it says TRESPASSERS WILL BE SHOT?" Alison whispered.

"I think it's the Arabic version for GO AWAY, SNOOPS," Eric shot back.

Gathering her courage, Alison doubled her fist and rapped first timidly, then firmly on the door. She stepped back and held her breath, glad that Eric was right behind her.

Someone inside the cottage was approaching the door. A turn of the latch, and the door swung open into the cottage. With one hand resting on the door-frame, a woman leaned out and, casually as any sub-urban housewife, asked "Yes?"

Surprised by the woman's easy manner, Alison stammered, "M-Miss Savina?" Her tongue felt stiff as dry leather in her mouth.

"Yes." The woman nodded and with a delicate forefinger pushed a strand of gray hair from her forehead.

"You're Americans, aren't you? I trust you have a good reason to come all this way to see me?" Her eyes widened in an expression of almost girlish delight that belied the signs of age in her lined face.

"I—I hope we're not interrupting anything. I mean, just breaking in on you like this." Alison's sweating hands tightened on the strap of her camera bag which she was trying to keep out of sight behind her back.

"My dears, in this wilderness I should regard all interruptions as God-sent. Almost all, that is." She spoke with a slight Slavic intonation to her words, that gave a musical lilt to the common English.

"You had best come in, then; I believe the wind's turning a bit chill." She opened the door wider and beckoned her unexpected guests to enter.

Alison and Eric shared a conspirator's wink as they stepped through the doorway and followed Anya Savina down a few broad stone steps.

"Come sit down. I don't even know your names."

She drew some plain wooden chairs close to the fireplace.

"My name is Alison Thorne, and this is my twin brother, Eric." Any other time Eric would have followed up his introduction with something charming or clever, depending on his mood. Alison was glad he remained silent and settled for a formal nod.

"And you may call me Anya. I grew tired of elaborate titles when I still was performing. Such tiresome nonsense. The shadow and not the substance. Have a seat and I shall put the kettle on. I imagine a cup of tea would be welcome to you; I know what a trek it is to come here." She strode away into the cottage's kitchen.

The intruders surveyed the contents of the room. It was plain but beautiful with well-placed Oriental carpets, a concert piano, and many shelves of books. Alison leaned forward to examine the titles of those nearest her. Many titles were Russian, but there was what seemed to be the complete set of Leo Tolstoy's work in English. A few more had on their spines faded gilt lettering in Cyrillic or Greek alphabets.

Miss Savina came back into the room from the kitchen. "Now then, my young friends," she said, sitting down across from them, "let's talk."

She appeared to have the same manner of speaking as Brother Thomas—the ability to draw a stranger into a conversational web as though they had been close friends for years.

"How old are you? I take you for about eighteen."

"We're sixteen actually," said Alison.

Eric smiled obligingly. Small talk was Alison's specialty.

"Ah." The older woman leaned back in her chair and placed the tips of her fingers together into a cage of thin ivory. She seemed to be thinking about her own youth.

"And may I assume Brother Thomas, my dear friend and protector, told you how to find me?"

"He did," Alison said. "We thought he was very nice."

Miss Savina smiled. "He is very nice, *and* very intelligent. But I'm surprised he didn't seem odd to a couple of young persons who have come traipsing all this way, just to talk to an old woman."

"I think you should know he was in sympathy with our reasons for coming," said Alison.

Miss Savina's smile indicated a wait-and-see attitude.

"Suppose you tell me, my young friends, what it is that you've come all this way to find out from me?"

Eric squirmed as the pianist's penetrating eyes looked in his direction for an answer.

Alison proceeded to give almost word-for-word the reasons she had listed for Brother Thomas. Miss Savina was keenly interested in their relation to the man who was the Vice President of the United States, and understanding of their feelings about losing their privacy. She broke in now and then with an anecdote of her own.

But at the point of their real reason for coming—

the Tolstoy assignment—she grew tense and restless.

"We are here," Alison said, "to ask about your father and his relationship to the great Russian writer."

"Indeed," said Miss Savina. Her eyes narrowed as she stiffened in her chair.

"You said in an interview on the eve of your retirement—an interview that was printed recently in *Arts in Review*—that you had in your possession some correspondence dated from about 1868 between Tolstoy and your father. That was about the time Tolstoy was writing *War and Peace*."

Anya Savina interrupted sharply.

"I have always regretted mentioning my father's name in that interview. It had not passed my lips during all the years since I defected to this country. It is useless to ask me about this matter."

The sudden coldness of her expression drained all the warmth from the room. Alison was stunned at the sudden change from friendliness to clear hostility.

"But—I thought—we thought—you might be glad to let us see them and perhaps translate them for us. It would give a unique touch to sort of validate our research."

Miss Savina made a sharp gesture for silence.

"My father was arrested on Christmas Eve in Leningrad along with other members of Russia's religious intelligentsia. He spent many years in Siberia where he saw many things. There are reasons it is not safe to mention his name."

"But surely you knew that his name would appear

when that interview you gave was printed," Alison pleaded. "What about the photos that show you in retirement—standing here in your cottage by the fire."

"Photos? What Photos?" Anya Savina's anger flared. "I never allow photos to be taken. I chased away a pest with a camera not long ago."

"I'm afraid he got the shots he wanted, anyway," Eric said. "He used a telephoto lens. Here, see for yourself." He took the copy of *Arts in Review* from Alison's hands and handed it to the Russian pianist.

The older woman's face paled to ashen gray as she looked at the magazine photos. The change made her seem even older and more fragile.

"This—this is a crime!" she finally said, scornfully tossing the magazine away. It took a moment for the steel to come back into her manner.

"It is a crime, I tell you—" In the kitchen the boiling tea kettle began to shriek in an idiot counterpoint to her anger.

"You must leave now," Miss Savina said coldly, rising from her chair. "These things are not to be spoken of."

"I don't understand. Why—"

"Go now." She strode to the cottage door and flung it open. "I tire easily; my age does not permit these interminable questions."

Eric took Alison's arm and headed her toward the door. "Perhaps we can talk again some other time," he suggested diplomatically. Alison was dazed with the sudden turn of events.

"No." The woman gave a quick, brutal shake of her head. "Do not return. You must forget this absurd inquiry of yours. My father's name is never, never to be spoken of."

They were barely outside before the door was closed firmly behind them. The click of the latch turning came from the inside, and the curtains were tightly drawn.

5 • Secret Cult

As the rain started to fall, lashing the Isle of Skye with the cold wind from the ocean, shades were drawn across the windows of another small, isolated cottage not far from Anya Savina's. A man's figure moved swiftly and quietly in a room's semidarkness. He strode with quick, sure steps to a closet, drew out a battered suitcase, carried it to a wooden table, and set it down on its side. Pulling out a chair, he sat down and opened the suitcase.

The contents contrasted sharply with the shabby outside. Most of the space was filled with a short-wave radio transceiver, coldly functional and military-looking in its dark metal chassis. Its combination head-set and microphone was fitted with an encoding/decoding scrambler device. The man drew out a coiled wire from the suitcase, then reached down and plugged it into a small socket hidden in a crevice in the floorboards. The socket in turn led to an antenna wire concealed in the cottage rafters. Small red lights glowed on the radio's panel as the man flicked on its switches. No sound came from the headset; whatever signal the radio was set to receive was not yet being sent.

As the man waited, he took a gun from the suitcase's smaller compartment—a Czech-made Scorpion machine pistol with folding shoulder rest and silencer. An assassin's weapon, quiet and deadly. Smoothly, with all the signs of long practice, the man broke the gun open. Taking a soft rag and small tools from the case, he began cleaning and oiling the dissembled pieces.

Presently, a crackle of static sounded from the radio. He took one hand from the half-reassembled gun and slipped the headset and microphone on. Making a few fine adjustments on the radio's dials, he spoke into the microphone.

"Go ahead," he said, his voice breaking the room's silence.

His hands went on assembling the gun as he listened to the voice coming in on the headset. He murmured, repeating words from the message.

"Yes," he said. "Two Americans . . . observed talking to Mullington about what? . . . Anya Savina . . . of course . . . and something to do with notes? . . . Are you certain they said notes? . . . Very interesting."

His eye caught a spark with the last part of the message. There was a muted click of metal as he snapped the last piece of the gun into place.

"No," he spoke clearly into the microphone. "There's no need to contact central headquarters. I have the situation under control." He reached into the suitcase and brought out a box of bullets. Carefully, he began loading the lethal tapering cylinders into the gun's clip.

"I'll take care of them," he said, pushing the full clip into place.

Far across Scotland, another figure sat in an Edinburgh hotel room. A silver-headed cane leaned against the wall by the door. The old man, his twisted leg stretched out to one side, leaned close to a small fire. Its dancing light was the only source of illumination in the room.

His veined hands prowled through a sheaf of photos. The pictures were of a woman in a cottage with Oriental rugs on the floor.

I have found her at last—there is no mistake. His face twisting with stifled rage, he crumpled the photos into balls of black and white, then tossed them into the fire. Their edges curled, became ash; gray, chemical-smelling smoke filled the room. More photos followed, and shadowy negatives on top of that.

I've paid that photographer well for these, he thought as the fire licked them up. *And a bonus to tell me who else comes asking about them.*

The old man drew a deep breath, steadying himself from his toxic rage. He reached down one hand caressing a slender dark shape that curled at the base of his chair. Two points of light reflected the firelight up at him.

"Soon," said the old man softly. "Soon."

All evening the storm dashed its sheets of rain against the windows of Mrs. Morland's bed-and-breakfast lodging. In her bedroom, Alison sat shivering. Her feet were clad in thick argyle socks and her hands were wrapped around a steaming mug of Earl Grey tea the old landlady had offered.

Alison sipped the dark brew slowly, letting her memory play back its record of the events of the disturbing day. Around her, the house creaked underneath the force of the storm.

She had gone over and examined every detail with Eric until he had begged for mercy. Nothing that they could come up with could shed any light on Anya Savina's puzzling behavior. The trigger seemed to have been the mention of her father's name—but what would there be about that subject that his own daughter would find so abhorrent?

Yet there had been something else. A current of fear was mixed in those angry tones, and it was sparked off by the photos. Could it be that Anya was afraid of being identified as her father's daughter?

Alison yawned as a wave of fatigue washed over her. The hiking was enough to tire anyone, much less the mental effort it took to try to unravel the mystery. Of one thing she was sure—she would not go back home without reaching her goal.

As Alison put her tea tray out in the hall, she saw a sliver of light under the door of her brother's room. She rapped softly on his door.

"Eric? It's me, Alison."

Alison heard him pad across the floor and unlatch the door.

"Come on in." Eric pulled the door open. "I wanted to talk to you anyway. I just thought I'd have to wait until morning to do it."

She followed her brother into the room and saw that his backpack was laid out on the bed. A couple of half-folded sweaters and pairs of socks were beside it. Everything else that Eric had unpacked when they had arrived at the bed-and-breakfast lodging was tucked back inside the backpack.

"Going someplace?" asked Alison, glancing from the pack on the bed to him.

He nodded in reply. "Yep," he said, picking up one of the sweaters, folding it and sticking it in the pack. "That's what I wanted to tell you. I'm going to Edinburgh in the morning." The rolled-up socks followed sweaters into the pack.

Stunned, Alison sat down on the edge of the bed and stared at him.

"Why, Eric?" she asked finally.

"I think we ought to cool it for a few days, Alison. It's a sure thing Anya Savina isn't going to help us, and I think we ought to let the dust settle before we go back to Brother Thomas, who might."

"So you're not saying we should abort the mission?"

"No, Sis, I don't think so. I'm only saying I think we should lay off for a few days," Eric answered as he zipped his pack shut.

"You know, Eric," Alison reminded him, "Dad wants us to stick together while we're over here. Just in case. . . ."

"Yeah, I know," Eric said as he put the pack on the floor and sat down beside his sister. "But it's not like I'm leaving the country or anything. Edinburgh is just a couple of hours away on the train. I won't be far away."

"I suppose not," reflected his twin.

Secretly Alison was beginning to wonder if Eric's decision had anything to do with Katy MacLeod. "Are you going to see that girl?" She asked teasingly.

"Well, if it really bothers you, why don't you come along with me?" Eric replied, ignoring the question. "Simple solution to the problem. That way Dad would be pleased, and you'd have nothing to worry about."

"I can't do that!" Alison lashed back angrily. "I'm not finished with what I came here to do. I've already put too much in it to drop out now. Besides, it's for both of us!"

Eric's shrug suggested a no-win situation. At least he had offered to take her with him. He tried again.

"I said I didn't think we should drop it, Alison. Just cool it. We could come back after a couple of days in Edinbugh."

"No," Alison said flatly. "I've got to stay here and follow it up. You go to Edinburgh."

Already Alison was beginning to see the positive side of the whole idea. There was no doubt she would have to go back to the Tolstoyan Community. With Eric out of the way, she could move any time and in any direction she chose.

"Okay," Eric said, smiling at her. "I'll phone you here when I get to Edinburgh and let you know where I'm staying. That way, you'll be able to get hold of me if you have to."

"Good! If I finish things up here real soon, I could meet you there."

He nodded. "Sure. Maybe take in a few sights before we have to head home. We haven't really seen much of the rest of Scotland."

"You'd better get some sleep, then," said Alison, "if you're going to be taking off in the morning. The weather's pretty lousy." Her sudden flare-up of anger at her brother had faded as quickly as it had come.

Alison said good night and went back to her own room. Dressing for bed and listening to the rain spattering on the shutters over her window, she wished she had not snapped at Eric the way she did. Actually, she was of two minds about his leaving for Edinburgh the next day. For some undefined reason, she would have felt better with him nearby. Maybe some of Anya Savina's unexplained fear had rubbed off on her.

"There shouldn't be any problem this time of the year," said Eric next morning as Alison waited with him for the bus to Armadale. "Now that the tourist season is over, there should be plenty of bed-and-breakfast lodgings in Edinburgh, too. I'll let you know as soon as I've found out where I'll be staying.''

Privately, he was already questioning his sudden decision. Was he crazy to go all that way in hopes of finding Katherine MacLeod—even when he didn't know where she lived? His only clue to aid him was folded in a neat square and tucked into his shirt pocket. Well, he'd enjoy touring the Edinburgh area anyway, he decided. But her good company could make it more interesting. She probably knew a lot about the historical significance of the city and surrounding countryside.

"Sure glad it stopped raining," said Alison beside him. The sky was still a sunless, mottled gray as the tail end of the storm passed over on its way north. "I was afraid it was never going to quit."

"What's your worry?" asked Eric. "How wet could I get aboard a train?"

"Who's worried about you?" Alison retorted. "I'm the one who's going to be slogging around in the mud here—and there's enough of it already!"

With a low grinding of gears, the bus pulled into view.

"Catch you later, Twinny," Eric grinned, lifting his pack by its straps.

"May the Lord watch between you and me, while we are absent, one from the other." The twins almost instinctively grasped hands and repeated the old Hebrew blessing. Family tradition had instilled these words within them for moments of parting.

98

As the bus lurched forward, Eric reached into his pocket and took out the folded sheet of paper Katy had handed to him in the tea shop. One corner of it was torn off where he had scribbled the information she had wanted. He had folded up the sheet of paper, and stuck it into his own pocket without realizing it. Their conversation had distracted him, and apparently her as well, for she hadn't seemed to notice him keeping it either.

It was only when he got back to his lodging that he found the paper in his pocket. Simple curiosity had made him unfold it and read it instead of throwing it away. After a few minutes, though, he was glad he had done so.

The paper was a mimeographed flyer listing upcoming events at the High Kirk St. Giles in Edinburgh, the largest Protestant church in the city. Along with the details of the regular services, a series of choral evenings was listed with several different guest choirs from local churches in Scotland. Some of the dates were already past, but one had been heavily circled with a red pen. It was one for that very evening! Eric would have only a few hours from the time he arrived in the city until it would be time for the choral performance to begin.

He had no way of knowing if it had actually been Katy who had circled the date on the paper, or if she even intended to attend the event. Worse still, would she think of it now that she no longer had the piece of paper to remind her?

Why was he following Katherine MacLeod to Edinburgh? A whim on his part? He had enjoyed her conversation, if for no other reason than that she seemed to be interested in the same things as he was.

Do I have to have reasons? He asked himself as he settled back into the worn plush seat. And why do I feel like a traitor to Alison? It wasn't my fault our research bogged down yesterday.

After seeing Eric off, Alison wandered along Broadford's central street. She had made up her mind the night before that she was going to keep working on the Tolstoy research in spite of Anya Savina. But now that it was the next day she was somewhat at a loss as to how she was going to go about it.

Should I go back alone and try to talk to her again? Alison thought as she walked along. In fact, she doubted if she'd get the door opened before it slammed in her face again.

Should I talk to Brother Thomas at the Community again? He had been so intent on guarding Anya Savina's privacy against unwanted intrusion, that if he was told that the aged pianist had tossed Alison out of her cottage, he most likely wouldn't tell her anything more, either.

It was certainly a tough problem, trying to determine what to do next. Alison was lost in thought and prayer for guidance when the sound of a car horn, like a nasal duck, broke in on her. She glanced up and saw the battered Austin sedan.

Trevor Nevis leaned across from the driver's side and waved out the window at her.

"Hello!" He called cheerily. "How are things going?"

By this point, she welcomed a break for a chat.

"Oh, fairly well, I guess, Mr. Nevis," she said, leaning her arm on the Austin's low roof.

"Trevor," he corrected her. "Fairly well, eh? When people say that, they usually mean 'not so well.'" He switched off the car's engine and pulled on the parking brake.

"I was about to stop and pick up a little morning tea. Why don't you come along and tell me about it? By the way, where's your handsome bodyguard?"

"He's off to Edinburgh for a few days." Alison answered, and immediately could have bit her tongue for saying so. One of the things her father kept telling her was not to be so trusting of strangers.

Shortly, seated at a table in the near empty dining room of one of Broadford's small hotels, Alison was plunking a couple of sugar cubes into a dark, steaming cup. Crumbling them with the point of her spoon, she said, "I thought you only came into town once every two weeks. At least that's what the lady at the tourist office said."

"That's right," said Trevor, stirring his own cup. "But actually, I was a bit worried about you and your brother, as I would be about any strangers wandering around Skye who didn't know the countryside. Hiking around these hills can be very dangerous, especially in the kind of weather we had last night. I was afraid you and your brother missed the postal bus and decided to walk back to Broadford. So, I thought I'd come into town and check to make sure we shouldn't send some search parties out looking for you."

Alison wasn't sure whether he was being playful or serious. She decided to reply as if he meant it.

"Well, that was kind of you to go to the trouble. But please don't worry—we'll try to be careful while we're here."

"Don't let my warnings scare you," said Trevor. "It's really a grand island for exploring. You really ought to take the hike out to Loch Coruisk, over past Elgol."

"Loch Coruisk?" said Alison. "I've never heard of it."

"Oh, it's a grand place," said Trevor. "The wildest and most remote loch in all of Scotland. It's nowhere near the size of Loch Ness. Lies right at the foot of the Black Cuillins, the steepest mountains in all of Scotland. Matter of fact, the terrain is so rugged that British mountain climbing teams practice on them before trying the Himalayas."

"Sounds fascinating," said Alison, sipping her tea. "How do you get to this loch?"

"Oh, it's a bit of a hike, all right. First you have to take the postal bus out to Kilmarie, which is just a little fork in the road. A foot path leads off from there. You cross over one range of hills and down to a little bay called Camasunary—there's an abandoned farmhouse there, and a few lost sheep still wandering about in the fields.

"Then the path continues around the cliffs of Elgol overlooking the sea until it comes to Loch Coruisk itself, just off a little sea inlet. The path is narrow, but not too tricky except in one spot just before you get to the loch. The people here on Skye call it the 'Bad Step.' It's a large boulder that sticks out from the cliff face and completely cuts off the path. There's no way around it except for two cracks that run across the boulder. You stick the toes of your boots in one crack and the tips of your fingers in the other, and inch your way around the rock while hanging out over the sea. It's a drop of a hundred feet or so to the water."

"Wow," said Alison. "Sounds kind of dangerous to me."

"It is scary, especially when the weather turns bad on you. Then the rock can get pretty slippery."

Alison visualized the large rock blocking off the pathway on a rainy, cold, gray day. She shivered at the thought.

"I don't think there's a sight anywhere in the world to match those desolate, still waters stretching out to the towering black mountains."

He fell silent, his gaze on the scene inside his memory.

"It sounds as though you really know this island well," said Alison.

"It's just that I've poked about a bit since coming here about a year ago from London."

Something about his mentioning London rang a faint bell in Alison's mind, something beside his clipped British accent.

"You know," she said, "I've had the strangest feeling that I've heard or read your name before. But for the life of me, I can't remember where."

Trevor smiled. "It's possible. If you read newspapers and magazines about the classical arts, it's very likely you might have come across my name on a few pieces."

It dawned on her then, like a light being switched on.

"Oh—Trevor Nevis. Now I recognize your name. You're the London reviewer who does a regular column—"

"Former reviewer," he corrected. "I gave up the post when I left London. I couldn't very well report on the London scene if I wasn't there, now could I? I've pretty much given up my writing career."

"You're not writing anymore?" asked Alison, astonished. "But why?"

"Oh, the usual reasons. Combat fatigue, as it were. One morning I woke up and decided I'd had enough. I sent my last column in and abdicated my role on the London scene entirely. I've been relaxing and nursing my battle scars here on Skye ever since. Can't say I miss very much of that other life of mine."

"Well, I suppose I can understand that," said Alison. She was thinking of her involvement in her grandfather's campaign and being able to see from the inside the pressures that can hit when you're in the public's eye.

"Enough of that, though," said Trevor. "It's all past history. How are you getting on with your own project? Did you talk to Anya Savina yet?"

Alison almost dropped her tea cup as she stared at him in amazement. "How did you know about that?"

He smiled.

"Elementary, my dear Alison. It's not hard to figure out when a couple of young internationals show up on the Isle of Skye and look for a ride out to the Tolstoy Community. I mean, there have been others, and that's the usual route they take to find Miss Savina. That's how I went about talking to her."

"You've talked to her? When?" Alison was shocked at having her plans so easily penetrated.

"When I first moved here to Skye. I had vague plans of doing a book about her, but when I saw what a private sort of person she was, I gave up the idea."

"Yes," said Alison, "she is kind of reclusive. I'm afraid I didn't get very far with her at all."

"I suppose you asked her about her father, and she showed you the door? Oh, don't look so shocked," said Trevor upon seeing her expression of surprise. "It's not that hard to guess. You're lucky you didn't ask about her husband!"

"I didn't even know she was married," Alison said dully.

It was almost too much to handle, these continual surprises about this man seated opposite her. She never took him to be a Tolstoyan, but to find that he was formerly a well-known London music critic was somehow bizarre.

"Anya was married to Petros Rascomine," he was saying, "a disciple of the founder of the Mullington Barakha Community, as it was then called. "He's dead now. Buried in a little field that runs right to the edge of the cliffs overlooking the sea. He is said to have been the greatest male dancer of his time. Or maybe of all time."

Alison was confused.

"But why was he attracted to the Barakha Community?"

"It was after he had given up the art to seek for what he called 'spiritual answers.' That quest led him through the remote reaches of Central Asia, from the Hindu Kush to the steppes of Siberia."

"Was he a lot older than Anya?"

"Not old enough to be her father—but almost. Petros Rascomine was in an area of Asia called Kazhiristan just before the Communist revolution hit Russia."

"Why did Petros Rascomine's spiritual search take him to Kazhiristan?" Alison asked, fascinated at the flow of information.

"Kazhiristan was a center of great religious activity, and the strongest of the Eastern groups had ritual dancing as the central sacrament of their religion.

You can understand how this would interest Rascomine."

"That explains it, of course," Alison broke in.

"The Kazhiristan religion was an offshoot of Islam that blended with it some elements of the Eastern Orthodox Church as well. In fact, participation in ritual dancing led by priests was almost like a sacrament."

Alison's eyes were riveted on Nevis' face. For no reason at all, she began to feel there was going to be a price to pay for the information he was giving her.

"For believers of the Kazhiristan faith," Nevis continued, "participation in the dance helped to ensure their place in eternity after death. Petros Rascomine became a follower and settled down in Kazhiristan to record these dances in notation form to help spread the religion abroad."

The steamy tea room, the remote sound of pounding waves, and this incredible story about Anya Savina's husband gave Alison the feeling she herself was in another time frame.

"What a story!" she said finally. "Why wouldn't Anya let you write it?"

Nevis shrugged.

"Petros Rascomine," Nevis' lowered voice began to sound sinister, "was the only person ever known to record those religious dances. The notations of them have suddenly become as valuable as mideastern oil!"

"I don't understand."

"Look here," said Nevis frowning. "I wouldn't tell you all of this if you weren't already interested in

Miss—Mrs. Rascomine. Maybe you haven't told me why you really came to see her. But here's the point—because of those rare notations, she is in great danger."

"I did get the impression she was terribly afraid of something. I thought it was an association with her father's home," Alison offered.

"You are quite right. She has used her stage name for many years, because those she fears know that the only daughter of Valentin Sorovin married Petros Rascomine."

Alison was about to ask Nevis why he was passing all this information on to a comparative stranger when he spoke again.

"Tell me, when you were at the Tolstoyan Community, did you talk to the one called Brother Thomas?"

She nodded.

"And did he appear interested in why you wanted to see Anya Savina?"

"Very—"

Trevor put his teacup down and folded his hands on the table. "I'll tell you," he said in a low near whisper. "I've had growing suspicions about Mullington and that little group of his."

"But I thought the group was disbanded," said Alison. "At least only a few of them are there now. We saw only one other person there—an assistant of his in the print shop."

"Groups like that have a way of being different from what they seem to be on the outside. I've reason to believe the Tolstoyan Community is a front, that the Mullington Barakha Community is not disbanded. It's not the benign little religious organization they pretend to be."

"What do you mean?" asked Alison. "What are they then?"

"I have some journalist friends in London who had spent some time assigned to their newspapers' Middle East bureaus. I asked them about the Mullington group, and they sent me some very interesting information. Take a look at these." He reached into his coat pocket and drew out a sheaf of yellow papers. Alison took them and leafed through them. They were cable messages from London, most of them headed Reuters; she recognized the name of the main European news agency. The top cable read TREVOR: ADVISE EXTREME CAUTION DEALING WITH MULLINGTON GROUP STOP IMPLICATED IN BEIRUT ASSASSINATION PLOT STOP DETAILS FOLLOW STOP. The rest of the cables told of similar suspicions that were ascribed to the Mullington group. Alison handed the cable messages back to Trevor, feeling faint. She could tell that the blood had drained from her face.

"There's evidence," Trevor went on, "that the organization is actually an offshoot of the Eastern religious order that was dominant in Kazhiristan before the Russian Revolution turned everything there upside down. Mullington and his followers are said to be fanatical adherents to that religion. They would kill to get hold of Petros Rascomine's dance notations."

"The notations? But—but why?"

"To you and me," said Trevor grimly, "the notations might be only of artistic value. But they apparently mean something else to Mullington and his group. You have to remember that those dances were a central part of the Kazhiristan religion.

"When the fighting broke out in Kazhiristan," Nevis continued, "nearly all the high priests whose duty it was to teach the dances were killed. By the time the new government was formed the Kazhiristan religion was without its primary ritual, and thus powerless. That's why the notation of the dances made by Petros Rascomine would be so valuable to Mullington and his group.

"The present government in Kazhiristan is a pro-Christian, pro-Western one; but there are strong memories among the people of the old religion. If the Mullington Barakha Community could get hold of the Rascomine notations of the sacred dances, they could return to Kazhiristan and start a movement that would put them in complete control of both the religion and the politics of that area. So you can see how much those dance notations would mean to Mullington and his group—and what they would do to get them."

"If all that's true," said Alison, "no wonder Anya Savina would be scared about anyone finding that she had the notations. But why would she stay so close to Mullington?"

"Perhaps," said Trevor, "she reasoned that if she fled Skye, the Mullington group would know she had the notations and would therefore pursue her across the face of the earth to get them. By her staying here on Skye, they probably believe she doesn't have them."

Alison fell silent, letting Trevor's startling theories sink into her brain. It was all so much more complicated and dangerous than what she had originally expected to find on Skye. Her thoughts whirled in confusion as she tried to sort through the maze that had been set before her.

"Tell me," asked Trevor Nevis, leaning toward her, "how did you find out Anya Savina lived on Skye?"

"There were some photographs," she explained, "in an American magazine. Here, I'll show you." She reached down into her bag and handed him the magazine.

"Hmmm." Trevor studied the pictures. "It's only a matter of time until these come to the Mullington group's attention. When they see these pictures, they will have to act. Anya Rascomine might be in worse danger than I thought."

"It's too late," said Alison. "I already mentioned the pictures to Brother Thomas—at least that's who he said he was—when I was out there asking for the way to see her."

"That complicates things, then." Trevor's eyes narrowed in concentration. "There's no way we can go to the authorities just yet. If we don't have any hard evidence about the Mullington group's intentions, they could just play innocent until the heat's off, and make their move then."

"What can we do then?" Alison asked.

Trevor pointed to the photographer's name in the magazine. "Look—I know this guy. Leonard Trent—he used to do some stage photography in London. Now he's located in Edinburgh." Nevis hesitated and stared off into space as though the plans he was about to describe were being slowly formulated as he spoke. "How about your catching the night train to Edinburgh and looking him up? Find out if he's been contacted by anyone. Get their names. The Mullington group might have tipped their hand enough to do something about them before they have a chance to move on Anya Rascomine. I can stay here on the island and keep an eye on the situation. I'll call in the police if I see them starting anything."

The plan seemed fuzzy to Alison, but she nodded her head. Her heart was racing with the sudden turn of events; she wished she could set out for Edinburgh immediately instead of having to wait for the evening bus to catch the ferry at Armadale. She would have suggested phoning the photographer for the information, but if she went to Edinburgh she might be able to find her brother and talk the whole affair over with him.

"All right," she said. "I'll go back to my lodging and get my stuff together."

"Good," said Trevor. "We're going to have to move fast. He pushed his chair back and stood up from the table.

"May I keep this?" he asked, picking up the magazine.

Dumbly, Alison nodded. He turned and quickly strode out of the dining room.

A short while later, a figure entered a farmhouse in the Skye countryside. He pulled a battered suitcase from a closet, set it on the table, and opened it. From the compartment beside the shortwave radio he drew the Czech Scorpion pistol, gleaming in the light coat of oil over its metal surfaces. He gave it a final inspection, pulling the fully-loaded ammo clip with quick, practiced movements, then pushed it back into the gun. Everything was ready to go.

The man laid the gun on the table. From his coat pocket he drew a folded magazine, glanced at the photos of the aged pianist in it, then tossed it down beside the gun. A crooked smile formed on his face, the smile of one whose plans were going well. Very well indeed, thought Trevor Nevis, pleased with himself.

6 • *Ambushed*

Alison's heart was pounding with the sudden turn of events as she headed for her room at Mrs. Morland's. Her thoughts were still racing to adjust themselves to the harsh situation into which Trevor's words had cast her.

Thomas Mullington, the head of a fanatical Eastern cult? Implicated in murders? And the religious dance notations of Petros Rascomine, the key to a possible takeover of power in Kazhiristan?

Alison's impulse to call the local police and tell them of the situation was stifled by the warning Trevor had given her. She wished she could talk to Eric. Between the two of them, she knew they'd be able to figure out the best course of action to follow.

For some reason, she felt an unaccountable anxiety about Trevor's plans to handle the situation, but she decided to put it out of her thoughts. After all, she told herself, the concern Trevor had shown for Anya Savina's safety was as great as Alison's own. If she started to doubt Trevor without any specific evidence to the contrary, then she would really be lost in a hostile world without friends. That's how paranoids must feel all the time, she thought grimly. I don't want to end up like that.

The phone was ringing as Alison turned up the path to Mrs. Morland's.

"It's for you, dearie," the red-cheeked landlady told her as she opened the door. Alison hurried to the hall phone expecting to hear Eric's voice.

"Hello—"

"Is this Alison, Eric Thorne's sister?" a lovely Scottish voice asked a little shyly.

"Yes, it is," Alison answered, trying to fight back the thought that Eric was in some kind of trouble.

"I'm Katherine MacLeod—in Edinburgh. Eric may have mentioned me. We were out near the Tolstoyan Community a couple of days ago. Perhaps he told you. I was hoping to speak with him but I'm told he's not in. Would you give him a message for me?"

"Certainly," Alison responded, debating whether to tell the girl Eric was on his way to Edinburgh. She decided against it.

"Tell Eric that a professor of mine at the university who saw my photographs of the standing rocks was curious about the markings. I only got a fraction of them in the shot, but he says it looks like a code to unlock some system of language."

"Yes," Alison said. "Please go on—"

"Well, Dr. Hudson says if he could see a shot of the complete stone he'd try to work out the combination. I thought it might be helpful for your research."

"Thank you very much, Katherine. We appreciate your interest. I'll tell Eric you called," she responded matter-of-factly and hung up the antiquated receiver.

"Oh, no!" Alison gasped when she realized what she had thoughtlessly done. She had not even asked for Katherine's address or phone. Would Eric know where to contact her? "How stupid of me!" She said aloud.

She glanced at her watch. The next bus to the ferry at Armadale would not leave until this evening, and it wasn't even noon yet.

If there was some way to get out to the Tolstoyan Community, she would be able to photograph the stones and observe the place from the hills above it—perhaps get an idea of what Mullington and his group were planning without them seeing her.

Alison pulled a tattered folding map of the Isle of Skye from her jacket pocket and studied it. The road that Trevor had taken with them the day before followed a long curving route out to the Community, but the map showed an old, unused sheep trail that cut directly across the range of hills and came out just above the settlement. The path would be steep, but Alison estimated that she could make it with enough time to accomplish her purpose, then catch the postal bus back to Broadford, and be back in time to get out to the ferry at Armadale.

She'd have to start out immediately, though. Without further hesitation, she got her camera and set out. She left the ocean behind her as she headed for the hills beyond Broadford.

An hour later, she was perspiring inside her parka despite the cold wind hammering at the face of the hills. Her hands were scratched from pushing aside the stiff brush and heather that had grown up over the sheep trail, and her hiking boots were caked with mud from last night's rain storm.

With a final effort, fingers and toes digging for holds, she scrambled up between the jagged boulders topping the ridge of hills. Crouching down behind one of the rocks, she cautiously leaned her head around and peered down into the valley.

The Tolstoyan Community was just below her, but because of the angle of the hill sloping down to it, she could see little more than a part of one building's roof and the usual trail of smoke rising from an unseen chimney. *Can't do much spying from here,* she thought.

Carefully, she mapped out in her mind the best route to reach the circle of standing stones. For most of the way along the valley's rim, she would be hidden by the boulders along its edge. But before she could reach the circle of stones, she'd have to cross a barren stretch where she would be visible to anyone downhill from her.

I'll just have to sprint that part, she thought. Taking a firm grip on her bag's shoulder strap, she set out for the distant stones.

With little difficulty she threaded her way through the boulders until she came to the last of them. She rested her palms against its rough surface and slowly inched her head around it. There was no one that she could see among the buildings in the valley below her. She took a deep breath, and broke away from the boulder, running for the safety of the stone circle.

The sloping hillside, boggy from last night's rain mired her boots, slowing her down. A patch of turf slid out from beneath her and she went down, hands and knees printing deep into the mud. With a quick glance down into the valley—still no one had apparently spotted her—she pushed herself up and ran harder for the circle. She dove the last few feet, landing on her side behind the nearest of the standing stones.

For several minutes, Alison lay behind the stone, catching her breath and waiting for the beating of her heart to slow down. Finally she rolled onto her stomach and crawled with her elbows to where she could peer around the stone. In the valley below her there was still no sign of human activity. Only a few of the hens continued their listless scratching about in the fields.

Made it—without being spotted! Alison congratulated herself. *Or at least, I hope not.*

She looked around the circle. The stones were set close enough together so she could move around among them and still be screened from the sight of anyone below. The shadows they cast formed a dark pool at the circle's center.

With occasional glances into the valley to see if anything was going on, Alison walked further into the circle. She understood now why Eric had been intrigued by this arrangement of carved stones. A brooding presence filled the circle's heart, as though old knowledge held inside the stones had sunk deep roots into the earth's lightless core.

She took her camera out of her bag and set the lens for its widest aperture in order to capture as much of the available light as possible. Then she set about photographing each of the stones, moving from one to another, standing at each one's base and focusing up on the barely discernible markings.

The last stone she came to was the tallest one in the circle, standing a full meter higher than the others. The inscriptions on it were much more extensive as well; Alison needed two shots to record them all on film. When she had clicked off the last photo she stepped back from the stone and gazed up at its towering silent presence.

Suddenly she felt an odd-stinging sensation on her cheek. At the same time, a short gray line etched itself into the dark rock just above her head. It wasn't until a fraction of a second later when the echo of a rifle shot ringing in the hills filtered through her that she realized a bullet had struck the stone, scattering a few sharp flecks of rock against her cheek.

Another shot rang out before she had time to think or move. A bullet dug into the ground several feet away from her, digging up a tuft of wet grass with its impact.

Alison's brain finally made contact with her limbs, and she dove for safety of one of the stones. She huddled at its base and scanned wildly about the circle. Someone was shooting at her—but from where?

She could see that no one had crept up into the circle without her being aware. The noise of the shots had the ringing quality of being fired from some great distance. Even if the stones hadn't blocked off any line of sight from the Community, the depth of the valley in which the circle was set would have made it impossible to place a rifle shot aimed from the settlement into the ground beside Alison.

That left only one possibility. She glanced up toward the high range of hills that loomed over the countryside from across the road. They stood high enough that the top of them commanded a view over the entire area that the stone circle was set into. A gunman could crouch among the boulders up there and target almost any point inside the circle.

She drew herself up into as small a space as possible, shielding herself behind the stone. Her mind raced dizzily. Why was someone shooting at her? Had one of the supposed Tolstoyan group spotted her when she had made her way to the stones, then circled around to the hills above her? She thrust the questions out of her mind without trying to answer them. Much more important was the question of how she was going to get out of the sight of the rifle stalking her.

She glanced at her watch. In a few minutes, the postal bus was due to go by on the road. If she could get out there and catch it, she would be safe. The gunman was obviously taking advantage of the isolation of the area to make his shots undetected. The presence of other people, even if no more than the mail carrier driving the bus, would frustrate that aim.

That seemed her only chance to reach safety. She couldn't go back the way she had come. Even if she got across the bare stretch before reaching the rocks on the other range of hills, she would still face the long hike back to Broadford with the gunman all the way at her back. Sooner or later, he'd have a clear shot at her.

But how to get out to the roadside? Once she left the security of the standing stones, she would be in plain view until she had gone nearly the entire distance to the gate. And then, if the bus was late, the gunman would merely have to come down from his perch on top of the hill to have another open angle at her.

If she stayed where she was, though, she could be kept for hours, frozen like a deer by the glare of a poaching hunter's flashlight. The night would descend upon her. The spectre of being stalked at night by the gunman moving unseen toward her in the darkness—a shiver of fear shook her body.

"Help me, Lord—what should I do?" She sent up an urgent prayer.

Slowly, Alison gathered her legs beneath her and leaned forward on the tips of her fingers like a sprinter at the starting blocks. As she dashed across to the next stone, another shot split the still air, followed by the whining ring of the bullet striking the face of the rock above her head.

The knot of fear in her stomach loosened its grip for the moment.

Stone by stone, she made her way to the edge of the circle. No more shots followed her; the gunman had apparently figured out her intent, and was waiting until she broke out into the open.

Leaning against the last stone, its great bulk shielding her from the rifle above, Alison fought to catch her breath while trying to estimate how far she'd have to run in the open before she'd be over the crest of the path leading down to the roadside. Twenty, twenty-five yards and then the downward slope of the path would put her beyond the angle of fire from the gunman's position on the hill. But first she'd have to get to that point. The yards stretched into miles as she estimated the distance she had yet to cover before reaching the road.

A low sound came out of the distance to her ears. It took a few seconds before she realized the postal bus somewhere on the road nearby and coming closer. In a matter of a few minutes, it would be passing the little wooden gate at the roadside. She would have to attempt the distance now or never. Would the gunman risk any more shots with others so close? Only one way to find out—she pushed herself away from the stone and dashed, head down, onto the winding dirt path.

Through the wave of adrenaline roaring from her brain to her racing arms and legs, she heard another rifle shot crack out of the hills. She lowered her head further and dove into a full-out slide, as though she were back in Ivy playing ball with her brother and going for second base. Her speed brought her just a few feet short of the path's crest. Stomach down in the path, she dug her fingers into the ground, pulled, and rolled shoulders first over onto the path's downward slope.

Silence blanketed the hills, broken only by the growing rattle of the approaching postal bus. Alison caught a glimpse of it on the curving road as she got to her feet and started to run down the path to the wooden gate, waving frantically to catch the mail carrier's eye.

The speed of the bus didn't diminish, and she was still some distance away.

"Hey! she shouted, pushing her voice past her laboring breath. "Stop!"

The bus rolled past the wooden gate, then abruptly braked to a halt, sending a clatter of loose stones against its rear fenders. She could see the driver's eyes following her in his rearview mirror as she ran up to the bus.

"Are you all right, Lass?" he said, pushing the bus door open. "You look as if you've seen a bit of rough hiking."

Alison scrambled up into the bus. She slung her bag off her shoulder and onto the seat next to her.

124

"I'm—I'm fine," she said, breathing heavily. She resisted the impulse to blurt out any of what had just happened to her. Trevor's warnings about Anya Savina's safety filled her thoughts. If she had any doubts about them before, this had dispelled them.

"I—took a bad fall," she said, brushing some mud from her parka.

Edinburgh was a city unfamiliar to Eric. Although the twins had traveled widely with their father, they had not been to the British Isles with him, for his consulting work in agronomy was done in underdeveloped countries.

I should have brought Alison's guidebook, Eric thought to himself.

Pack firmly slung on his back, Eric walked up the short road that sloped toward the city's train station. He could see to his right a towering fantasy of spires and gables like a cathedral tower that had been set down in a green expanse of park. That must be the Sir Walter Scott Memorial, he told himself. So that's Princes Street over there.

Gaining his bearings, his eyes swung to his left. There was Edinburgh Castle itself, the medieval fortress rising on the stone cliffs overlooking the town. The grim battlements and cannon turrets of the castle commanded a view over both the twisting lanes of the Old Town at its base and the straight geometric avenues of the New Town's elegant Georgian buildings.

With a little aid from the Tourist Centre, Eric

located a bed-and-breakfast lodging a few blocks down Hanover Street. The setting sun was turning the bottom fringe of the clouds red and gold by the time he had unpacked his bag and changed his clothes.

From a pay phone out on the street, he placed a call to Alison in Broadford. He registered a moment of concern when the landlady told him she was still out. Leaving his address and phone number for Alison, he hung up and started toward the Old Town and St. Giles cathedral.

He climbed the twisting street called the Mound that led to the Royal Mile running downhill from the Castle to Hollyrood Palace at its far end. Glancing at his watch, he saw that he was going to be late for the choral performance listed on the paper he had absentmindedly taken from Katy MacLeod. He hurried toward the dark shape of the High Kirk St. Giles looming on his right.

Mounting the wide stone steps, Eric straightened his tie and buttoned his coat. Faintly he heard voices massed in song. Trying to make as little noise as possible, he pulled open one of the massive wooden doors and slipped inside.

The vast spaces of the cathedral towered above him, all vertical columns of stone broken by high expanses of stained glass, dark now without the sunlight behind them to draw out the rich colors. Beyond the wooden pews the choir in white-collared gowns was ranked in rows.

Eric slipped into a seat at the rear and scanned the

small crowd in front of him. No one had turned around to look at him when he had entered. For several minutes as his eyes went over the backs of heads one by one, he began to doubt that Katy was there. After all, he had no assurance that she had intended to come here tonight. Even if she had circled the date on it, there was no way of telling if she'd remember it without the paper in her possession.

Then, when his heart had almost sunk to its lowest pitch, Eric spotted a cascade of reddish-gold hair in the front pew. He couldn't tell for sure, but it was enough of a hopeful sign that he could draw a deep breath, lean against the pew's low back, and patiently wait for the choral group to conclude its presentation.

Presently, silence refilled the cathedral's vast spaces, broken by the respectful applause of the small audience. Someone spoke a few words of thanks from the lectern, and with a shuffling of feet the people rose.

Eric threaded his way forward. The figure he had taken to be Katy's still faced away from him. She turned, her eyes widening when she saw him.

"Eric!" she gasped. "What are you doing here?" I thought you were still back on the Isle of Skye. In fact, I telephoned you there a few hours ago."

"Oh," he said casually, "I just happened to be in the neighborhood, so I thought I'd drop in." He broke into a grin. "Surprised to see me?"

"Well, yes, of course," she replied. "How did you ever find me? How did you know I was going to be here tonight?"

Eric reached into his coat pocket, took out the folded paper, and handed it to her.

"I see," she said. "Quite the detective, aren't you? Though I don't think I would have come all this way on a clue as slender as this one."

He shrugged. "Even if I hadn't found you here, I still always wanted to see Edinburgh. This was a good enough excuse to come here."

"You mean you've never been here before?" Her eyes brightened with enthusiasm. "Oh, Edinburgh's a wonderful city. I really envy you, seeing it for the first time."

Discovering they were almost alone in the cathedral, they turned and walked slowly up the nave.

"I don't suppose I could enlist your services as a guide, then?" asked Eric.

Katy smiled.

"I'd love to show you around. But my classes start up the day after tomorrow. I was planning on going out in the morning to do some sketching—" she snapped her fingers as the idea struck her.

"Say, there's something you might enjoy seeing."

"What's that?" asked Eric.

"I was going to go out to Melrose Abbey tomorrow. It's a lovely fifteenth-century ruin—Sir Walter Scott wrote a lot about it. You told me that you originally came to Scotland to see stone carvings, so you might find the Abbey especially interesting. Some of the columns have particularly fine detail on them." Katy touched his arm. "Would you like to come along?"

128

"Sounds great." Eric stepped with her into the chill evening air outside. "I think I'd enjoy that."

"Then it's settled," she said. "I can borrow my folks' car. I'll swing by wherever it is you are staying in town early enough so that we can get out to Melrose before anyone else does."

"I hope I'm not being a nuisance," Eric said hesitantly.

"Not at all," said Katy. "Actually, I had been thinking of you. When you showed up there at the High Kirk, it was as if you had popped right from my thoughts into the aisle."

The night train ride to Edinburgh had been exhausting for Alison. Stretched across an empty seat, her back pack lodged in the steel luggage rack above her head, she had been able to drift off into much-needed sleep for only a few minutes at a time. Then a replay of her running from the gunshots back on Skye would jolt her awake again, to stare at her frightened reflection in the train window filled with night.

Who could it have been? she puzzled for the thousandth time. *And why were they firing at her?* The most probable explanation, depending on what Trevor had told her, was that it had been somebody from the Tolstoyan group. Alison speculated that they might want to get anyone who knew Anya Savina lived there out of the way before they moved in on her themselves. And that would mean me, she thought. After all, I was the one who told them about the leak of her father's name and the magazine photos in the first place. They had been so trusting and talkative with old Brother Thomas. But how were they to know?

Morning came at last. The train pulled into the Edinburgh station. Before she did anything else, she wanted to talk this over with her brother. It seemed the authorities should be informed, but Trevor's warning that calling in the authorities too early might further endanger Miss Savina's life ruled out Alison's making any phone calls for outside help.

She headed for the Tourist Centre. Fortunately, the number of student tourists at this time of the year was small. The woman behind the desk recalled Eric from Alison's description of him. The address of the bed-and-breakfast house where he was registered was neatly written out for her, and the directions pointed out on the big city map on the wall.

After a check of her guidebook, she headed down Hanover Street, and within a quarter hour she had located Eric's lodging. But there her good progress stopped. The landlady reported that he had left earlier that morning. Alison quickly scribbled a note to leave for him, gave it to the landlady and headed back to the center of the city.

Her next step was to locate Leonard Trent, the photographer who had taken the pictures of Anya Savina. A few minutes in a pay phone booth and she had found his name listed, complete with an address for his studio not far away on Frederick Street. Fishing a few coins out of her pocket, she put through a call, holding her breath as she heard the phone ring-ing on the other end.

A click, and a man's voice came on. "Hello?"

"Mr. Trent?" asked Alison quickly.

"Yes, that's right. Can I help you?"

"You don't know me, Mr. Trent; my name's Alison Thorne. I wanted to talk to you about some of your photos that appeared recently in *Arts in Review,* a magazine published in the United States."

"Oh?" interrupted Mr. Trent. "Which photos are you speaking about? The Prime Minister at the cat show, or the blind channel swimmer?"

"Uh, none of those," said Alison. "Actually, I was thinking of the photos you took of Anya Savina up on the Isle of Skye."

"Oh, those! That's certainly an odd coincidence," he commented mysteriously.

"What do you mean?" Alison's heart raced faster.

"Look here," he said, changing his tone abruptly. "Are you here in Edinburgh?"

"Yes."

"Then why don't you come around to my studio and we can talk about it."

"Fine," said Alison. "I'll be there in just a few minutes." She hung up and hurried toward Frederick Street.

Soon she was standing at the street door of an old but immaculately clean office building. She pressed the little buzzer beside the brass plate with LEONARD TRENT, PHOTOGRAPHER engraved on it. A mo-

131

ment later, she heard steps coming down a flight of stairs inside.

The door pulled open to reveal a genial, red-bearded bear of a man. His large, blunt hands looked too clumsy to operate anything as fragile as a camera. A shop apron, stained with photographic chemicals, barely covered the front of his massive frame.

"Miss Thorne?" he said upon seeing Alison standing before him.

"Yes, that's right," she said. "Mr. Trent?"

He poked a wide finger through his tangled beard. "I wasn't really expecting anyone quite so young. You sounded very businesslike over the phone."

Alison followed him up the winding mahogany staircase to the top floor.

She felt at home among the clutter of a working photographer's quarters. Several tripods were racked against one wall. Camera bodies were lined up on top of a long work table. A system of cubbyholes with printed labels organized Trent's collection of lenses. Through another door, Alison could see the tanks and sinks of Trent's developing equipment, rows of chemicals in plastic jugs on the shelves above. In all, it was a working studio that Alison observed with envy.

"I'm afraid you'll have to excuse the condition of the place," said Trent.

Only after her initial glance around the studio did Alison see what he was referring to. Proof sheets were scattered over the floor in front of the gray file cabinets. Negatives were heaped in careless piles like dark leaves from storm-tossed trees. One of the file cabinets, all its drawers pulled open, had toppled forward from the imbalance.

"What happened here?" Alison asked.

The photographer shrugged his burly shoulders. "Someone broke in last night, though I can't imagine how—I've got double latches on all the doors and windows. Whoever it was went through my photo files like a madman, looking for something in particular. Quite a mess, isn't it?"

"What did he take?" asked Alison.

"Well, that's the reason I was so surprised when I heard you mention Anya Savina on the phone." Trent walked over to the mess, picked up a sheaf of proof sheets, and began disconsolately leafing through them. "As near as I can tell, all the intruder took were the negatives and proofs of Anya Savina that I took on the Isle of Skye. Nothing else."

"That's all?" Alison felt her heart catch a beat before going on. Could someone from the Mullington group—perhaps even the gunman who had stalked her—have come all the way to Edinburgh and done this? Who else would have such a driving interest in gathering all the available evidence on Miss Savina's whereabouts? Alison's mind whirled with the questions, repeating themselves over and over again.

"Before you got here," continued Trent, "I was beginning to think that perhaps you might have something to do with all this. I mean, you must admit it's rather odd that the morning after my studio is broken into, a total stranger comes along and inquires after the very photos that were lifted from here. But then when I saw you, I realized you couldn't be involved in the matter."

"How do you mean?" said Alison.

"My dear Miss Thorne," said Trent, smiling at her, "I am a professional photographer. It's a part of my business to keep up with who's making news in the world. As soon as I saw you, I recognized you as the granddaughter of the new Vice President of the United States. There was a picture of you just a couple of months ago in a magazine I sold some photos to. Now, how likely is it that the granddaughter of a U.S. Vice President would be involved in stealing photos?"

"Not very, I guess." Alison felt a bit of relief at being cleared of the photographer's suspicions.

"But tell me, what was your interest in seeing the pictures?" Trent asked with more than casual concern.

"Mainly," said Alison, "I was interested in finding out if you talked with Miss Savina, and if anyone has asked you about her, or about the shots you took."

"I doubt if I had more than a dozen words with the old woman," said Trent. "As soon as she saw my camera, she chased me right off. I think it was more out of spite than anything else that I took those tele-photo shots of her and sold them to that magazine. That was a bad move on my part; I rather regret it. But I'm afraid I'm rather fond of money—"

"You didn't answer my question about any other

inquiries you might have received," Alison persisted.

Trent looked uncomfortable, Alison thought.

"No others—" he said, squinting at one of the negatives and holding it up to the light of the window. He looked across the street to the park.

"I'm very sorry about this theft," said Alison. "Hope I haven't taken up too much of your time. You've got a lot of work ahead of you putting your files back in order."

"Oh, it shouldn't take too long. Everything's labeled. But before you go, Miss Thorne, would you mind?" Trent gestured toward his portrait setup with the blue seamless background paper.

"Even if you weren't a semi-celebrity, I'd like to take a few pictures of you. Very interesting bone structure you have about your face."

"I wouldn't mind at all," said Alison. "Then perhaps you could do me a favor as well."

"Anything I can do for you, I'd be delighted."

Alison fished in her bag and brought out an exposed roll of film.

"I took some shots of a stone circle on the Isle of Skye. The light wasn't very good, and I wanted to bring out the detail. Do you suppose you could run them through your darkroom for me?"

"No trouble at all," said Trent. He took the roll in his blunt fingers and disappeared into the other room. A short while later he reemerged, wiping his hands on his shop apron.

"I see what you mean. It took some doing on your

part to get as much on the film as you did. They turned out well, though, with a bit of pushing. The prints just need to dry a little." He motioned her under the skylight.

"If you step over here a bit, while I get my Graflex mounted—Won't take but a minute."

Soon after Trent had finished taking his photos, Alison was heading down the stairway from the studio, a manila envelope of the stone circle prints in her hand. She passed another phone booth and stopped to call Eric's lodging. He still had not returned, according to the landlady. Alison thanked her, hung up, and pondered her next move. Deciding to take the photos of the stone circle back with her to Skye, she stepped out of the phone booth and headed for the train station.

The greatest need was to get back and tell Trevor about the break-in at the photographer's studio. It might mean that Mullington and his group were starting to make their move. She would just have to make her decisions without her brother's help, after all.

The figure sitting on the park bench on Frederick Street drew his breath in sharply when he saw the dark-haired girl stride out of the building. His hands tightened on the silver head of his walking stick. He had seen the girl before, at the Armadale ferry dock on the Isle of Skye. Even then he had suspected her of having some connection with Anya Savina. The connection, though unclear, was solid in his mind. If the old man had had any doubts about the necessity of what had to be done with the girl, those doubts were gone now.

He congratulated himself for recognizing and capitalizing on Trent's weakness for money. The photographer had called him when he heard from the girl, and promised to contrive some ruse to delay her until he got there.

He shouldered his bag, his twisted leg dragging behind his cane's stabbing motions, and he made his way after the girl. When he was this close to accomplishing everything he burned for in this life, he could afford to take no chances.

7 • *The Knife and Its Master*

The drive from Edinburgh down to the ruins of Melrose Abbey led through some of the most beautiful scenery Eric had seen in all of Scotland. With Katy at the wheel of her parent's Rover, Eric was free to watch the landscape unrolling before his eyes.

The last rains before the winter snows had brought out a final blush of color in the heather blanketing the hillsides. The land itself was not the harsh craggy geology of the Highlands, with its rock-strewn cliffs plunging into the chill, dark waters of its lochs carved by ancient glaciers. Instead, the countryside was that of the Lowlands and border counties, less dramatic, but more soothing to the eye and restful to the spirit.

Though it was an ocean and half a continent away, in some respects the area reminded him of the hills surrounding the little Illinois campus town of Ivy where he had grown up. At this tail end of autumn, the same profusion of deep red and orange colored leaves spilled from the branches of the now-skeletal trees here as at his Illinois home. A wave of longing to be back there at this time of the year touched him now. *It's been quite a while,* he thought to himself, *especially if I count the time I was on the campaign trail with Gramps, since I was really at home.*

Katy pointed down a road branching off to the right.

"Sir Walter Scott's old home is down that way," she said. "Quite a place, though we won't have time to look at it today. He had it built to his specifications, and named it Abbotsford, because it was right on the spot where the monks from Melrose Abbey would cross the Tweed River as they went about their various priestly duties in the countryside."

"You know a great deal of the local history and everything connected with it," Eric said approvingly.

Pleased at his words, she gave him a sunny smile. "For me, Scottish history reads like a novel. It's not the dry sort of history you'd get with the Austro-Hungarian Empire or some other Middle European stomping ground. In those places it seems like all battles and no characters. I'll admit it's hard to figure out some events in Scottish history though, because there's a whole big streak of sheer lunacy that runs through it."

"Tell me more," Eric insisted.

"Byzantine history, I've always thought, is hard to understand because everyone there was so sneaky you could never tell who was on what side," she continued. "In Scottish history, half the events can only be explained by saying, 'At this point, everybody involved went crazy and did the following crazy things!' Why else would the conspirators who killed Mary Queen of Scots' husband, Lord Darnley, do it by blowing up the house he was in with gunpowder? Fireworks are one thing, but that's ridiculous. No, as much as I love this country where I was born, I'll have to admit that there must be something in the air that makes the natives go a wee bit daft.''

Eric chuckled at her long spiel on the peculiarities of Scottish history. She had become freer and more animated in her conversation with him. He had been so candid with her in talking about some of the things that were on his mind—all that business stemming from his sudden and unwanted fame—that it meant a great deal to him that Katy would open up in the same way.

"Not much farther to go," she announced turning the car off onto a side road. "We're almost there.''

The asphalt strip cut through a little village, no more than a collection of compact shops and a few surrounding rows of houses.

"This is Melrose proper," said Katy, "I'm afraid there's nothing remarkable about the town itself.'' She wheeled the car expertly through the narrow street crossing the postage-stamp-sized village center.

"And there's the Abbey, right over there," she said, pointing through the windshield. "You can just see its front facade through those trees.''

Beyond a cluster of tall larches, Eric could see the skeletal outline of the stone framework for what had been a circular stained glass window outlined against the gray clouded sky. The rough stone wall of the Abbey, weathered by the passing of the centuries, towered above the carefully tended, park-like green space around it, all square-cut hedges and dew-laden grass trimmed to a billiard-table smoothness.

"It must have been quite a sight," she commented, "back in Sir Walter Scott's time, when everything around here was a bit wilder than it is now.

'If thou wouldst see fair Melrose aright,
go visit it by the pale moonlight.'

"That's what Scott wrote in 'The Lay of the Last Minstrel.' There are some marvelously spooky prints in his study at Abbotsford, showing what the Abbey looked like at night back then—quite spectral. One could just imagine the ghosts of the long-dead monks filing in procession, chanting their vespers." She pulled the car up into a small parking lot a little way from the Abbey, and turned off the engine.

"Even like this," said Eric, "it's haunted-looking." The battered dignity of the stone ruins transcended its park-like surroundings, like an aged warrior-king brooding upon a polished throne. From where Katy had parked the car, a long row of tall stone columns, surmounted with weathered figures of saints, marched into the dark interior of the Abbey.

"Come on!" Katy pushed open the car's door on her side. "Let's go on in."

For a moment Eric hesitated. In the silence that lay heavily upon the morning, to intrude upon the Abbey's once-hallowed space seemed almost like sacrilege. But then, he reminded himself, it was a church, not a fortress. In the time when it had been alive and functioning, it had served as a refuge, welcoming all who came. He got out of the car and crossed the wet grass in Katy's footsteps.

"This was the nave right here," she said as they walked into the ruins. All was now open to the sky. Although much of the high stonework walls remained, the high vaulted ceilings of the Abbey had been destroyed and carted away. She pointed to the long row of columns, each forming at the base a square, stall-like shape.

"Those were the chapels," she explained, indicating the enclosures. "The noble families of the region around here each used one for their family burial place."

"Just how old is this place?" asked Eric as he gazed up at the towering stones.

"Oh, it was originally founded in the twelfth century, but there's only a section of one wall that dates back that far. I'm afraid the Abbey's been destroyed and rebuilt several times. It was right in the path of the invasions from England into Scotland. Most of what's here now dates from the fifteenth century. After that, no one bothered to rebuild it. As a matter of fact, the local villagers used the ruins as a quarry, taking away a lot of the stones to build their own houses. There wasn't the interest in historical preservation then that there is now."

"I guess not," said Eric. The apprehension that he had felt before entering the ruins had lifted like the mist evaporating from the surrounding hills. In its place came a respect for the long-dead monks' consecration to the praise of God and to the service of others.

"Here's what I thought you'd be most interested in seeing." Katy led him further into the darkest section of the ruins. The walls of the cross-shaped heart of the Abbey were still largely intact, including the base of the original tower. Consequently, most of the early morning light was shut out, plunging the transept spaces—the arms of the cross—into dim obscurity.

Eric's eyes were still adjusting to the lack of light when Katy brought him to a column that was higher and larger in circumference than the others.

"This is what's known as one of the 'curly kale' columns," she pointed out. "Look up there."

He raised his eyes as she directed, and saw nothing until a shaft of light broke through the massed clouds beyond the hills. The ray passed through the circular stone window framework high above the Abbey's floor, then fell upon the top of the column. A deep carved stone design of intertwined foliage was bathed in golden light.

Every detail, every small leaf and stem, twisted about the column as though it had grown there and then been turned into stone. But it was more than an imitation of the way the foliage looked in nature; the stone carver had captured the way the foliage felt to the soul, when the soul first saw God's creation and loved it.

Alison ran her eye down the table of arrivals and departures posted at the Edinburgh train station. The next train running to Mallaig and connecting with the ferry to the Isle of Skye wasn't leaving until later that afternoon. Nothing could be done about that; she would just have to wait, no matter how intense her fears of what might be happening on Skye with Anya Savina and the Mullington group.

Alison hauled her backpack to a wood-slatted bench, and sat down with an audibly grateful sigh. Somehow it seemed as if she had been running at top speed for days.

Her lack of sleep from the train ride the night before, plus the muted din of the station combined to cast a leaden fatigue over Alison. She was afraid, though, that if she drowsed she might sleep right through the departure time for the next train to Skye. To fight the growing heaviness in her limbs and eyelids, she took out the manila envelope that the photographer Trent had given her and examined the large black and white prints. She could see immediately that Trent was a real professional in the dark room; he had done an excellent job of developing the pictures for maximum contrast. In a sense, the pictures exceeded reality in the amount of detail they showed on the faces of the standing stones. The markings on the stones were now nearly ink black against the light gray background of the stones themselves.

As she leafed through the photos, studying the pattern of the markings, something about the lines and circles and odd-shaped marks teased her eye with a haunting near-familiarity. She understood why Katy's professor was intrigued. They were like unknown math equations, or a score for a yet uninvented music. How strange that there was no record of a study being done on the markings of these stones. She must ask Trevor Nevis about this. He'd probably know where she could find something. When she came to the photos of the circle's largest stone, the one where she had needed two shots to fit in all the markings, an idea—no more than a faint suspicion, really—raised itself in her mind like a flower uncoiling from the night.

"Please excuse me, Miss." A man's voice broke into her concentration. "I wonder if you could give me a hand with this."

She looked up and saw an elderly man standing before her. He was leaning his weight on a silver-headed cane. Beyond him, she could see by the clock on the station's wall that it was almost time for the train to Mallaig to leave. Quickly she stuffed the photos back into the manila envelope Trent had given her.

"I'm sorry," she said to the old gentleman as she tucked the envelope into her bag. "I was so preoccupied that I didn't quite hear what you said."

A thin smile creased the old man's face of wrinkled parchment.

"I was wondering," he said, "if you would be so kind as to help me carry my bag onto the train. I have an infirmity that makes it difficult for me." He took one hand from the silver ball of his cane and indicated his twisted leg.

145

"Oh, of course," said Alison. "I'd be happy to." The gentleman looked small and frail in his neatly tailored dark suit; she felt a little wave of sympathy for older persons who had to ask strangers for assistance on and off trains.

"What train is it that you're taking?"

"I believe they're just starting to board right now," he replied. "It's the one out to Mallaig that connects with the ferry to Skye."

"Then it's no trouble at all," said Alison. "That's my train, too." She stood up and slung the strap of her pack over her shoulder, then reached down and lifted the old man's bag from beside his feet. It wasn't very heavy, but for a moment she thought she could sense a subtle shift of weight inside it. With her free hand she gently cupped the old man's elbow.

"Shall we board?"

"Thank you," said the old man. "You're really very kind." As they walked to the train, he looked closer at Alison.

"You're not from here, are you? Your accent strikes me as being American."

"That's right," said Alison. "I was born in Illinois."

"The United States is one of my favorite countries," said the old man, smiling. "I very recently spent a bit of time there."

"Perhaps we can travel together," she suggested. "It's a long ride out to Mallaig. That'll help pass the time. My name's Alison, by the way."

"I'm very pleased to meet you, Alison. I'm Mr.

146

Croyden." The thin smile on his lined face grew a little wider.

"Yes," he said, "I would enjoy having a—conversation with you, Alison."

There was no difficulty in finding an empty compartment. Only a few passengers were aboard the train. The tourist season was over, and it was still too early for commuters. Alison slid open one of the small wooden doors, complete with its pane of glass, stepped in, and hoisted her bag up onto the shelf above one of the seats. She was about to do the same with Mr. Croyden's bag when he stopped her, laying his thin hand on her arm.

"Just leave it on the seat, please," he said. "I may need something from it during the ride." Dragging his twisted leg behind him, he entered the compartment and sat down, his arm resting easily across the bag.

"So, Mr. Croyden," she said brightly. "You say you were in the States a little while ago? What business are you in?"

The old man leaned back against his seat. "I deal in diamonds," he said, "and other valuables. But I was in the States on some personal business. Something I had been working on for years. It gave me great pleasure to finally achieve it." A thin smile played on his pale face as though it were the shadow of some ghostly memory.

Alison wasn't sure whether it was something she should ask about or not. Before she could decide what to say, Mr. Croyden spoke again.

147

"Would you like to hear about it?" he asked genially. "I'm afraid it's rather a long story, but then we do have a long ride before us. I'd really enjoy telling it to you, and you might find it interesting. In a way, it even concerns you."

"Concerns me?" asked Alison, puzzled.

"You see, it has to do with someone I believe you have an interest in—Anya Savina and her husband, Petros Rascomine." A strange tone crept into the old man's voice as he spoke the name.

Alison couldn't believe what she was hearing. What connection could this old man have with all of that?

"I know a great many things, young lady," said Mr. Croyden. "A great many things. And one of them is Petros Rascomine. I know how he betrayed someone who trusted him, how he sent that person to years of a living hell and to the edge of death itself. Oh, yes, I know a great deal about Anya Savina's husband."

The change in the old man's manner sent a shiver along Alison's spine. The genial figure was gone, replaced by what seemed an aging bird of prey, leaning forward with his hands folded on the silver head of his cane. Part of her feared what he might say about the long-dead Petros Rascomine. And yet, if it was the truth, she wanted to know.

"Tell me," she said quietly, as if the old man's voice had already created a hypnotic fascination for her.

"My little tale begins," said Mr. Croyden, "some time after Petros Rascomine had given up his dancing career. He wanted other things, he told people. He passed himself off as something of a mystic. Rascomine had traveled a great distance in the world, and was familiar with the languages and customs of certain remote areas in Central Asia. So it seemed like a sound idea for two young linguists to enlist his services as a guide."

"The expedition to Kazhiristan?" asked Alison.

"I thought you might know something about that, said Mr. Croyden. "But I know much more. You see, I was one of the linguists who went on that expedition."

"You!" said Alison. "Then you were the one who came back from Kazhiristan with him—"

"No." The old man shook his head sharply. "The other one—his name was Strother—he came back from Kazhiristan with Rascomine."

"But I thought one of the linguists was killed in the fighting that broke out while the expedition was there."

"I wasn't killed." said Mr. Croyden furiously. "I was betrayed—betrayed by my colleague Strother and the great religious mystic, Petros Rascomine! Framed and sent to prison because of them!"

"But—but how?"

The old man breathed deeply to dispel some of the anger that sent the blue veins pulsing at his temples.

"I wasn't the only one who suffered because of them, either," he said bitterly. "Strother and I both took our families with us to Kazhiristan, because we expected the expedition to last more than two years. My wife and little boy—he was only five then—they were lost, too, thanks to Rascomine."

He broke off, peering intently at Alison.

"Does my hatred surprise you? That I should despise the name of Petros Rascomine—does that seem startling to you? My hatred was all that kept me alive through all that I suffered. It was the heat in my veins when I was lost in the freezing snow; it was the bread in my stomach when there was none. And it became my child when I had lost all that was precious to me. Do you understand that?"

Alison was caught by the eyes staring so intently at her. "I don't know," she stammered. "How did Petros Rascomine betray you? And why?"

"The why of it is simple enough. He and Strother did it to save their own miserable hides. You see, when the fighting broke out in Kazhiristan, the rebels thought we were working for the government they were trying to overthrow. The government, on the other hand, thought our expedition was a front for Bolshevik agitation in the remote regions. Before we could clear out and cross the border, the Bolshevik-led group gained power for a brief period, and we were all arrested and taken in for questioning.

"Because we were innocent, I thought that I and my family had nothing to worry about. A few days later, I found myself on a train, traveling under armed guard into the depths of Russia. I never saw my family again. It's miracle enough when a man emerges from those prisons—what chance did a woman and child have? None, none at all."

"But what were you accused of?"

"Quite simple," said Mr. Croyden. "In order to divert suspicion from themselves, Strother and Rascomine told the Bolshevik group that I had been working for the Kazhiristan government, and that my participation in the expedition was just a front for organizing loyalist groups in the remote areas. That's all it took. Rascomine and Strother were taken to the border and released, and I was shipped into Russia. I found out the details of how they had falsely testified about me long after when I was rotting in a Siberian prison camp."

"But if you were innocent," said Alison, "why weren't you released?"

"I'm afraid the Russians had strange ideas about justice, especially in those years just after the Revolution when Stalin was in power. Innocence had very little to do with punishment. I wasn't the only one who disappeared into the prison camps, to be forgotten and to die.

"Anya's father was there. I knew Valentin Sovorin's daughter married Petros, but I didn't know where she was until that magazine interview was printed."

"But you're alive, Mr. Croyden," Alison interrupted. "Aren't you thankful for that?"

"I got out," said Mr. Croyden. "But survived? Only part of me did—the part that wants revenge above all else.

"Do you know anything at all about what life is like in a Siberian prison camp? The cold with nothing but sweat-stiffened rags between your flesh and the snow, the unending labor cutting trees or pounding out roads in the barren steppes, the meager rations of stale bread and thin soup, the barracks crawling with vermin and disease."

Alison could sense that Croyden was living the past in the present.

"Even now I sometimes wake up in the middle of the night and feel the bare wooden planks of a prison bunk beneath me and hear a fellow prisoner in the last stages of tuberculosis coughing his lungs out. The air thick with the sour sweat of unwashed bodies. Then I remember that I am out, and that I have a task still before me. Would you like to hear just how I escaped?"

"Yes," said Alison, watching the old man cautiously. The noises of the train rushing over its steel rails seemed very far away. "Tell me."

Mr. Croyden's hands knotted tighter on his cane's head.

"The work detail I was on was tree cutting. I was half blind from hunger and fatigue. My axe slipped and I struck myself in the leg—this leg here." He nodded toward the twisted limb.

"The bone was smashed, but the entire medical treatment consisted of swaddling it in rags to stop the bleeding, and dragging me back to the barracks to die. An injury like that is usually fatal in a Siberian prison camp. But something saved me."

"What?" said Alison. "What saved you?"

Was Alison imagining it, or was there a movement in the old man's case?

"An animal," said Mr. Croyden.

"I had saved it, and now it returned the favor. On a previous work detail in the forest, I had found it in its burrow, only a few weeks old. Its mother had died fighting off a wolf. I could tell from the blood and paw marks in the snow. It was an animal found only in the Siberian forests. The closest thing to it is what is known here as a fisher—something like a ferret or a marten, only larger.

"The Siberian animal is also more cunning and vicious. It has to be, to survive in those barren regions. The one I found would have died out there in the snows if I hadn't carried it back to my barracks, tucked inside my rags where no one could see it. Something about it touched my heart—perhaps I felt it was as abandoned and alone as I was."

It was apparent to Alison that the only tenderness left in the old man was for the strange animal he described.

"I kept it hidden in my bunk, and fed it crusts of bread from my own scanty rations, moistened in the soup they gave us. And it lived. It grew, became larger and stronger. I turned it loose outside, but it returned to the barracks. It would lie curled against my chest, its warmth mingling with mine. I loved it very much. And when I looked into its yellow eyes, it was as if I felt something pass from me to it, some deep spiritual connection between its soul and mine." He paused as if deep in thought for a moment.

"Then what happened?" asked Alison.

"I lay there in my bunk," said Mr. Croyden, "a

fever growing from the shock of my smashed leg, and when I woke, the animal was gone from my bunk. It knew I was dying, I thought, so it left me. I lost all hope then. I lapsed into another fever-wracked sleep, but when I woke a small object lay beside my head. It was a bird the animal had killed and brought to me. It was going to feed me because I had fed it!

"I ate the birds and scrawny forest rabbits it brought back to me. At first raw. Then later, when I had regained a little strength, I would wait until the others left on their work details, crawl to the tiny barracks stove and cook the small carcasses there. The meat was better for me than the watery soup and moldy bread.

"Gradually I realized," Croyden said, "the animal could read my mind—animals are much more sensitive that way than people. Everyone has heard stories of dogs that seemed able to carry out their masters' wishes without being told. This animal and I were much closer together than any man and his dog.

"Soon it began to bring me other things I wanted—first a piece of string, then money filched from the guard's quarters, even clean bandages from the prison infirmary. That's when I started to think of escaping."

The bizarre story was momentarily interrupted by the conductor's arrival to check tickets, but the narrator continued without missing a beat.

"So one morning, the camp awoke to find the night guard at the entrance gate dead, his throat ripped open by a wild animal, and one of the prisoners, the one with the crippled leg, gone."

"The animal—the one who had fed you—killed the guard?" Alison asked in disbelief.

Mr. Croyden nodded quickly. "An animal like that is a natural killer; it had to be in order to survive. And mine was a very good killer. It could slink within inches of a man without being seen, then spring for the throat, its claws catching hold of a man's clothes as it darted up the body. Very sharp teeth; within seconds it was all over. So you see, I had the perfect ally in my pet. It could go where I could not go, do what I could not do, see where I could not see."

"And so you escaped," said Alison. The grim story sunk ice into her spirit.

"Yes, I knew that a tribesman who lived near the camp would take escaped prisoners west to the Finnish border for a price. I paid my way with the money the animal had stolen from the guards' quarters. The tribesman I hired turned out to be a drunkard, and I had to get rid of him. My pet was handy in doing that. We went on by ourselves. I lost the trail in a blizzard, and had to abandon the troika. Three days later, I crawled into a little Finnish village, half-frozen to death, but the animal was still with me. He'd always be with me—we were part of each other.

"I gradually regained much of my ruined health. The years had passed since Strother and Rascomine had betrayed me in Kazhiristan. I had no desire in my life but to find them and destroy them wherever they might be. I headed south and wound up in Amsterdam, the center of the European diamond trade. Again, the animal came to my aid. It could find its way into any locked storeroom in the city, and then return to me with a flawless blue gem tucked in its cheek. Soon I had a small legitimate trade of my own. I prospered and lived quite frugally.''

For a moment, Croyden's mind relaxed. A slight shift of weight in the bag at his side brought him back to the present.

''I soon learned that Petros Rascomine had died here in Scotland while I was in Siberia. He was beyond the reach of my vengeance. Strother had covered his trail well. But I had my vengeance. Before the animal got to him in the luxury apartment he thought so impenetrable, he knew who it was that had come for him.''

The old man closed his eyes and breathed deeply. The violence of his tale had caused his hands to tremble. But not for long. He opened his eyes and focused his somber gaze on Alison.

''Well?'' he said sardonically. ''What do you think of my little story? Do you need proof of it?''

One hand grasped the bag's zipper and pulled it open.

Moving slowly under a dreadful fascination, Alison leaned forward. Her heart froze as she saw within the bag's dark recesses, a still darker shape curled about itself. The jet-black fur caught a glint of light as the two yellow eyes looked back at her without blinking. A lip curved upward in a silent snarl, revealing a row of razor-sharp teeth, as the muscles beneath the sleek hide tautened as if to spring.

"So you see," said Mr. Croyden, "it is true, after all. This is a very long-lived animal. And the thirst for revenge in my heart has kept it from aging. I may be a feeble old man, but I have an unfailing weapon. And I will have my revenge against Petros Rascomine."

Alison stared at him.

"Petros Rascomine is dead."

"Part of him still lives," said Mr. Croyden grimly. "I discovered it quite by accident when I had almost given up the search. I must kill that part of him which remains."

For the first time, Alison could see the blinding light of insanity burning in his eyes.

They spent the whole day at Melrose Abbey.

At a small outdoor stall they bought cheese and fruit, then hiked up into the hills overlooking the village.

They had spoken only a few words since the initial wandering through the ruins. There was little need for words. Katy was lost in concentration with her sketch pad, and Eric was occupied with the carved stone ornaments, climbing about the ruins.

Eric was the one who broke the silence at last.

"You know," he said as his gaze lifted from the valley to the gathering storm clouds, "I think I've found what it was I was looking for when I came to Scotland. I'm really glad you brought me here."

Katy turned toward him. "And what's that?" she asked.

"It's hard to put into words," he said slowly.

"Somehow, the unknown stone carvers found a way to create something that lasted. Even with the Abbey now in ruins, its beauty is still here.

"That's true," said Katy. "But, you know, even stone finally perishes and is gone."

"Yes," Eric answered. He turned his gaze from the Abbey to Katy's listening face.

"What really lasts is what you do for others. Take these stone carvers. The stones they worked on are passing away with time, but the effect persists on the people who through the centuries have seen and been inspired by what they did here to honor God."

Katy listened with interest.

"These carvings represent the work of a lifetime for many of the monks. I have a feeling they worked gladly on these tedious, intricate designs, as one way of expressing their worship and love of the Lord. And, as far as I can see, not one of them signed his name, or received special recognition for his faithful work. None of them as an individual became a famous celebrity."

Katy smiled in understanding. Eric wasn't sure he had found the right words to express his thoughts, but he gratefully accepted her willingness to listen.

"That's one reason I wanted to bring you here, Eric. I think it's a very special place. I'm glad you felt some of the same feelings here that I did."

The first drops of rain fell before they reached the car. As they looked back at the ruins of the Abbey, the rain was darkening the stones, each drop moving with the slow chisel of time.

8 • The Knife Strikes Again

The rain spattering on the window of the compartment blurred the darkening landscape. Inside, Mr. Croyden's soft voice continued its downward spiral into madness.

"You see now, don't you?" he was saying. "I lost everything, my wife and child, everything that mattered in my life, because of what Strother and Rascomine did to me. I found Strother at last and took my revenge on him but Petros Rascomine was beyond my reach. How do you destroy a man already dead?"

"And then, while I was in the United States taking care of my little business with Strother, I came across a magazine. I don't even know why I picked it up in the first place. But it held the key to completing my revenge."

"I discovered," continued Mr. Croyden in his taut, crazed voice, "that the wife of Petros Rascomine is still alive and living here in Scotland. If she had been satisfied to remain Anya Savina, I would never have known. But she mentioned her father, Valentin Sovorin, and spoke of some notes of his she was keeping. I knew instinctively that she also was keeping the sacred dance notations that Petros Rascomine, her husband, had taken with him from Kazhiristan.''

The old man leaned back in his seat, smiling as if he were relishing his expected triumph.

"Petros Rascomine lives on," he said quietly, "as long as those dance notations of his still exist. His wife could decide any day to give them to the public, and then his fame would be reestablished. He would become famous. He would be immortal, and I'd never be able to destroy him.''

Alison broke her silence, her voice straining in her clenched throat. "But you can't do that," she protested. "Those notations are important works of art.''

"I care nothing for that," said Croyden fiercely. "I will have my revenge. The religious notations of Petros Rascomine will be destroyed. His wife and all others who have any knowledge of them will die too. I have already located Anya and made my plans to kill her.''

"It will be easy enough: as though some wild animal had come upon her in her isolated cottage. I have waited to set my little vengeance here against her until I could go to Edinburgh and discover if anyone else was interested in the photo.''

"So you're the one that broke into Trent's studio!" said Alison.

The old man shrugged. "That was not necessary. I had already purchased all the photos. That was simply a ruse to confuse and hold anyone who came inquiring about the photos there until I signaled Trent from the park. It was easy to see he was a man who couldn't pass up a bribe."

Alison remembered Trent's own admission of that with disgust.

"When you came out of Trent's studio, I was rewarded for my pains. It was then I remembered seeing you at the Armadale dock where I heard you talking about notes and Anya Savina. Overhearing that made me suspicious immediately. Then when I saw you were the one coming from Trent's studio, my suspicions were confirmed: you were in search of Petros Rascomine's dance notations! You even look like a dancer."

Croyden paused to catch his breath.

"She gave them to you, didn't she?" he accusingly eyed her for any sign of confirmation.

"No, she did not!" Alison shot back. "And I am not a dancer. When my brother and I came here, we knew nothing about this Petros Rascomine and the religious dance notations you're talking about. We came to find—"

"Oh, naturally you'd deny it," said Mr. Croyden. "I expected that. But whether she gave them to you or not, you realize of course, that I can't take any chances on it. You do understand that, don't you? If there's any chance at all that you have Petros Rascomine's dance notations and I let you live, then I haven't completed my task. I won't have destroyed Petros Rascomine. I'm sorry, but you realize what has to be done, don't you?"

The impact of the old man's words, like the point of a knife working slowly beneath the skin broke through Alison's dizzied thoughts. Her breath tightened around her hammering heart.

"You're insane," she whispered as her back pressed against the seat as far from him as it could go.

"Perhaps," said Mr. Croyden softly. "But then I have reason to be."

The bag, thought Alison suddenly. *I have to get away from it.* But the bag beside Mr. Croyden was already gaping open and empty! The animal, with its sulfurous yellow eyes and gleaming razor teeth, was already out, moving silently and unseen in the compartment.

The paralyzing fear that had been growing while she listened to Mr. Croyden's insane monologue now gave way to a surge of adrenaline. She darted from her seat to the compartment's door but not before something sharp caught at her sleeve.

Black shining fur and the gleam of teeth—

A tearing noise came as the nylon fabric of her parka was ripped open and the animal's teeth sank into the thick down padding. She jerked her arm convulsively, and hurled the animal's dark shape and sinuous weight back into the compartment.

Frantically, she tugged the door open and half fell into the corridor. As she bolted toward the door, she saw no other passengers in the car.

163

The latch of the exit door slipped beneath her trembling fingers. Unlatched, it balked and refused to slide open more than a few inches. Bracing both hands and the point of her shoulder against the door's edge, Alison pushed frantically.

She sensed that the train was slowing. A sign outside flashed by with the name of a stop on it. *A station!* she thought.

Even as she struggled with the door, Alison prayed. "Lord, if I ever needed you, I need you now!"

She was terrified at the thought of being trapped inside the train's narrow, enclosed spaces. Meanwhile, Croyden's animal was making its calculated, gliding way toward her.

A sudden movement of the train loosened the door. There was a rush of wind in her face. The door opened. She was free!

As the train slowed, she saw from the corner of her eye a concrete loading platform. Without waiting for the train's full stop, she jumped toward the platform from the metal steps of the coach.

For a moment she thought she would be able to stay on her feet, but then lost her balance, falling and sliding across the concrete, her arm scraping across its rough surface.

Gasping for breath and conscious of a dull throb of pain where she had landed on her arm, Alison rolled onto her knees and hands. About twenty yards down the platform she could see the passenger car, its door swung open, come to a halt.

Looking around quickly she saw the platform was deserted. Even the small ticket office at one end was closed. It was a small country station, nothing more than a platform and wooden posts with carved Victorian ornaments. The storm rattled its downpour of rain upon the corrugated metal panels of the station's roof. If this station was like others she had seen in the Scottish countryside, Alison knew that a village should be nearby, perhaps just a few yards down a road. Or it could be as far as a mile away.

It was her only chance. She scrambled to her feet and ran for the station's exit.

The narrow road fronting the station curved away in two directions. Alison could see no village lights in either distance. Brushing strands of wet hair from her face, she noticed the blood oozing from her scraped arm. Frantically, she took the road to the right. There was no time for figuring out which direction to go. Mr. Croyden and his deadly pet could be only a few minutes behind her.

The road curved and mounted beneath her running feet. As its angle grew steeper, she could see it like a dim ribbon before her, cutting a range of hills. She turned around and saw a cluster of village lights and buildings half a mile away in the other direction. Panic gripped her mind as she realized she had made the wrong choice.

Then she saw it. Between her and the village lights someone was moving up the road toward her. She saw a glint of light strike something silver. Alison knew that another form, smaller and darker, had caught the scent of her trail.

There was no hiding place on the road's flat surface. She thrust herself through the thick mass of brush alongside the asphalt, the foliage catching at her face and shoulders like tiny claws. In a crouching run, her fingers outstretched to catch herself from falling, she made her stumbling way up the rocky hillside.

The rain washed her footing from beneath her, slowing her down. Her breath burned agonizingly in her lungs.

Suddenly a stone, loosened by the rain, broke from beneath her foot. She slipped backward, sliding a few feet down the face of the hill. At the same time, she heard another sound cutting through the pounding roar of the storm—the sound of an animal's whining snarl.

Alison rolled onto her side and saw the small dark shape, its yellow eyes like points of fire in the rain, gaining up the hillside. Farther downhill, Mr. Croyden was pushing his way through the break she had made in the brush beside the road.

Then the animal was upon her, leaping across the last few feet between them. Instinctively, Alison brought up the padded sleeve of her parka to protect her face and throat. Again, the sharp points of teeth and claws dug into the nylon fabric, tearing it away in shreds.

Her free hand caught the animal's middle, the rope-like muscles twisting beneath the sleek, wet fur. She tried to push it away, but its grip on her parka was too strong. The effort whirled her about on the muddy

166

ground so that she was facing directly downhill.

Through a haze of panic and rain, she saw Mr. Croyden climbing toward her, his crippled leg dragging behind him as the cane stabbed deep into the muddy ground. The madness that drove him on masked the reality of a terrified girl struggling with cutting death on a rain-soaked hill. The only sounds Alison heard were the teeth slashing closer to her arm and throat and the hoarse panting breath of the climber as he struggled up the steep hillside.

Suddenly a red face emerged—an unhealthy red from a pounding convulsive heart. Then it turned white, as if all the blood had drained from it. For a moment the burning look of vengeance changed to one of puzzlement, then deep pain. Croyden stiffened, and with a muted gasping cry cut short, he toppled forward.

The force bearing down into Alison's arm and throat stopped suddenly. The animal's dark shape crept slowly away from her and toward the crumpled figure. As Alison watched, the animal crawled up into the knot of the old man's arms and huddled against the body, its eyes staring straight ahead. The old man's heart had burst with the struggling climb up the hillside and the furious madness that had impelled him there.

The animal seemed transformed by the old man's death. It was no longer the sleek, smooth-muscled creature Alison had first seen in the bag on the train. It looked smaller and very old, curling up to die with the master it had served.

Alison, numbed by exhaustion and fear, stumbled

back down the hillside and away from the scene. She reached the road and headed back for the train station.

From the schedule posted on one of the station's walls, she saw that the next train was scheduled to stop in an hour. She could still reach Skye that night.

In that station's empty restroom, Alison stuffed her parka, torn beyond repair, into the trash can. Fortunately, her sweater beneath was still dry. With a handful of paper towels she washed her face and mopped the mud from her jeans. She did all this automatically, not letting her mind rest upon any of what had happened. She could not risk breaking down into the shaking tears building up inside her, not yet.

In a farmhouse on the Isle of Skye, a man sat at a telephone waiting for his call to go through.

"Mrs. Morland?" he said into the phone. "Trevor Nevis here. I just wanted to remind you to give the young lady staying at your place that note I left with you. Yes, to Alison, please. It's rather important— you'll be doing us both a favor, I'm sure. You won't forget, will you? Thanks again for your trouble. Goodbye."

As he turned from the phone, his hand brushed against a waterproof leather pouch revealing the hard outlines of the gun he had cleaned and readied. He picked it up from the table and slid it into his inside jacket pocket, then smiled tightly to himself.

Everything was now ready for Alison's return.

A porter aboard the earlier train had noticed her bag abandoned in the passenger car and turned it into the Mallaig stationmaster. Alison was able to claim it with little difficulty before she boarded the ferry to the Isle of Skye.

By the time her bus reached Broadford, it was close to midnight. She had called ahead from Mallaig, and Mrs. Morland promised to leave the front door unlocked. The rain had slowed to a monotonous drizzle by the time she got off the bus. She made her way through it and slipped quietly into the darkened guest house.

Inside, she mounted the hallway stairs to her room. Her mind was such a whirl of questions and frightening memories that she almost missed the sealed envelope taped to the bedroom door. She pulled it off and closed the door behind her.

Weak from fatigue, she clumsily tore open the envelope and took out the folded paper. *Alison*—it read. *Don't worry about Anya Savina, I've made arrangements for her—but I'm afraid that the Mullington group suspects you of interfering with their plans. You should be safe for tonight, but we'll have to hurry. I think I can get you safely away. Take the postal bus in the morning to Kilmarie and then take the foot trail to Camasunary. I'll have a small boat at the inlet there to take you back to the mainland. Stay calm and don't tell anyone. The Mullington group must not find out that you've been warned. Trevor.*

Alison sat down on the bed, the paper dropping from

her hand. She had escaped from Mr. Croyden and his dark, shining-eyed animal only to land back here in the heart of danger. Fear like an icy wave struck her in the pit of the stomach. She curled up on the bed, squeezing her eyes shut against unseen things moving toward her. First the gunman on the hill above the standing stones, then the animal's flashing teeth and claws in the rain. When would this nightmare ever end?

Again and again she voiced her prayer for guidance and protection to the Lord. "And bring Eric back soon, Father! Thank you!"

She was not at ease in trusting Trevor's plans for getting her off the island but she knew of no option. The fatigue that had built up inside of her took over finally and she slept fitfully. Inside her feverish dreams, the fear still ran after her in the dark.

She woke with the gray morning light sifting in through the bedroom window. For a moment she gazed blankly at the clouded sky, until the memory of all that had happened flooded in upon her. She sat bolt upright and checked her watch. She'd have to hurry to catch the postal bus as Trevor's note had directed her. Pulling on another sweater for warmth, and grabbing a waterproof nylon windbreaker from her neatly compact backpack, she dashed down the hallway stairs and out the front door.

Within a few minutes, she was seated on the postal bus rattling along toward the hills, the only passenger aboard. The driver let her off at Kilmarie—marked by a stone bridge over a small stream and a few houses near the crossroads. He pointed out where the trail to Camasunary began.

"Be careful, lass," he warned as he put the bus back into gear. "Looks like bad weather for hiking."

The chilled wind scudded the banks of gray clouds through the sky above her. She climbed over the low fence and started up the footpath toward the crest of the hill.

It was a good half-hour's walk to the top, but from there she could see down the other slope of the hill to the small, abandoned farmhouse that marked Camasunary. The tall stalks of yellowing grass and weeds ran almost to the water's edge. From her high vantage point, she could also see the figure of a man sheltering his back from the wind against the side of the farmhouse.

"That's Trevor," she said aloud as she started down the path. "His plan must be going all right!" She looked around for the boat, but she wasn't able to spot it.

Emerging from the base of the hills, she hurried across the fields through the crowded stalks. As she came closer, Trevor moved toward her.

"Alison," he said, smiling. "I'm glad you got here."

"I got the note," said Alison, out of breath from her rapid progress down the hillside. "Are we going to leave for the mainland now? How did the Mullington group find—"

She froze when she saw the object in his hand.

"What—what's that for?" she asked, astonished, looking at the unmistakable dark, oiled metal instrument. Trevor, still smiling, leveled the gun at her.

"There's going to be a slight change in plans, Alison." He stepped quickly across the few yards separating them.

"But—but what are you doing?" Alison's eyes flicked from the dark circle of the gun's barrel to his hardened eyes.

"It's really quite simple," said Trevor, still with mock gentleness. "I'm afraid I've misled you rather badly. You never had anything to fear from old Mullington. He's just a silly old fool, muttering his religious platitudes to himself in his little hideaway. He has no group of fanatical assassins chasing after you *or* Anya Savina."

"But the cablegrams you showed me," said Alison.

"Forgeries, I'm afraid. They're easy enough to come by when you work for the people I do. You see, I've been a Soviet agent for years. All the time I was in London I was the main conduit for stolen military secrets being sent to the Kremlin. I actually left London because my cover as a music critic was in danger of being blown. I wasn't lying when I said that those religious dance notations of Petros Rascomine were very valuable. And that is the little matter my Russian employers wanted me to handle here on the island."

"I don't understand," interrupted Alison limply. "What value could the dance notations have for the Soviets?"

The gun pointing at her did not waver.

"Oh, it's quite simple. Kazhiristan lies right on the border of the Soviet Union and holds one of the potentially richest oil-producing regions in the world. The present government is strongly pro-Western. But, if the sacred dances of the old Kazhiristan religion could be reintroduced, this religious group could become strong enough to overthrow the pro-Western government.

"The Kazhiristan followers would be definitely pro-Soviet," Nevis continued, "especially since it will be the Soviets who return the dance notations to them. So, you see, these notations could be the key to turning over the entire balance of power in the Middle East area."

Alison rubbed her throbbing forehead and prayed. Only God could help her now. She could not run anymore.

Trevor continued speaking.

"While in London, I reported to the Kremlin the rumors that Anya Savina might have the notations in her possession. They sent me here to find out if it was true, and to get them from her without arousing attention. I had not been able to discover whether she had these or not. But now I know she does, because you have been heard talking about some notes that she has."

"But it's not the dance notations! I came to Skye to see the notes and letters her father received from Tolstoy!"

"Come now. Don't try to cover it up, Miss Thorne," Nevis responded coldly. "You see, old Mullington's helper in the print shop, Alfred, really works for me. He keeps a close eye on who the old man sends to see Miss Savina, then radios me with the details.

"Now that I'm sure the old woman does indeed have the notations, I can apply more—shall we say, forceful methods to get them from her. However, I can't leave any loose ends like you around. I'm afraid something is going to have to be done about you, Alison."

"But—why are you telling me all this?" So much had happened in the last couple of days that Alison had no trouble in believing Trevor's revelations about himself. Only the fact of her own death being coldly calculated baffled her.

"Perhaps I'm just overly sentimental," said Trevor, stepping closer with the gun and raising it. "But I just don't think somebody should have to die without knowing why. Especially when I enjoy telling them."

A sudden thought sparked Alison into action. Although her self-defense training at Central High last year was not intended to handle armed assailants, what alternative did she have?

"One thing, Mr. Nevis," she began calmly, "You may need me around to decode what I have here in my pack. You had better think twice about the implications—"

Alison continued to speak as she slipped the pack off her shoulders and let it drop to the ground behind her. She waited for Nevis to respond by coming around behind her to check its contents. As he moved around to her right, with a quick judo kick her boot caught Trevor heavily in the knee, half-turning him about and throwing him off balance. The gun spun from his grip and fell a few feet away.

Without looking back, she plunged into the tall grass and weeds beyond the abandoned farmhouse and kept running. Behind her, she could hear a moan of pain as Trevor fell toward an outcropping of jagged rocks.

The field suddenly ended at the edge of a stream running down to the inlet. A few yards away a small suspension bridge, wooden planks strung on steel cables, swayed over the stream. A dirt path on the other side of the bridge climbed upward. Alison ran to the bridge and crossed it, the planks bouncing up and down beneath her boots.

For the second time in less than twenty-four hours, Alison found herself running from death. There was no protective foliage on the hill. A few more yards, and she would be racing along the crumbling edge of a narrow path cut right into the face of the cliffs overlooking the sea.

She heard a voice shouting from behind her. Looking back, she saw Nevis standing at the bridge, the gun clenched in one hand.

"The trail dead-ends at Loch Coruisk," he yelled. "You can't get away now!" He started up the dirt path toward her.

She fought the panic rising within at hearing the

taunting words. While she was in motion, it seemed she had a chance somehow. Blind to what lay ahead, fear pushed her on along the path that curved around the cliffs.

Leaning against the sloping ground beside her for balance as she ran, Alison caught an occasional glimpse of Trevor in steady pursuit. The rain was falling heavily now, making it difficult for Nevis to get a clear shot at her from that distance. At the same time, it made the footing more dangerous beneath her boots. Several times she felt the edge of the narrow trail crumble, and heard the loose rocks tumble down the cliff face before splashing into the ocean below.

After what seemed an eternity of running, Alison looked ahead and saw that she had nearly rounded the mass of cliffs. The abandoned farmhouse was lost to view.

On this side, the cliffs were much rockier; and the narrow path threaded through a jumble of massive boulders that spilled down to the sea. Much farther ahead, the path sloped downward to a little strip of rock-strewn sand that separated the ocean from a darker body of water beyond. There the path ended— at Loch Coruisk itself. Towering beyond the dead-still waters were the jagged shapes of the Black Cuillin mountains, their snowy heights masked by storm clouds gathered about them. A more effective barrier could not be imagined—beyond them there would be no passing.

But that was still in the distance. Alison, stumbling

along the path little wider than her boots and with a straight drop into the frigid waters beside her, suddenly halted at the sight before her. It was the Bad Step that Trevor himself had told her about. A massive boulder covered the path and jutted out over the ocean. There was no way around it.

She came up against it and stopped. Her eyes searched for the cracks in its surface he had described. She scrambled across it with her hands until her fingers caught at a broken ridge of stone, barely wider than her fingertips. Bringing the toe of her boot up against the rock, she scraped it downward until it found the other crack running parallel to the higher one. Then she took a deep breath, pulled herself up onto the stone's face, and started to inch her way across the face of the rock overhanging the ocean.

Clinging like an insect, she made slow progress, sliding one hand and one foot at a time along the cracks, then drawing the other limbs to herself. Her cheek, pressed against the boulder, caught the flow of rain washing across its surface. She turned her head and saw Trevor coming along toward the boulder. She would be an easy shot from there.

Desperately, Alison reached farther along the crack. The toe of her left boot lost its hold in the lower crack and slipped free. Clinging only by her hand hold and one foot, she scrabbled with her left foot at the rock face. Finally it found the crack again. The effort put her around the curve of the boulder, just out of Trevor's angle of fire from the path.

She continued inching around the giant rock until she saw the edge of the path on the other side. A little more, and she had made it. She loosed her grip of the crack and dropped down onto the dirt trail, then ran down the incline toward the loch. Now Trevor was starting around the boulder, his jaw set and grim, the pistol tucked into his jacket pocket.

Jumping from one rock to another, she reached the little strip of sand cutting the loch off from the ocean. There was no path beyond it!

She looked wildly about her for some avenue of escape. Had Trevor spoken correctly; the base of the Black Cuillins on the opposite shore of the loch blocked any way of getting out. There was not even a hiding place, just barren rock running down into the dark water.

"God, what now?" she prayed. "How do I get out of here?"

She ran to the water's edge, searching for some crack in the barren, rain-battered landscape large enough for her to squeeze through, to hide herself in—

"You see?" The voice came from behind her. It was not taunting now; it was grim and exhausted from the chase along the cliff face. "It was all just a waste of time. You could have saved us both a lot of trouble."

Back against the edge of the loch, Alison watched Nevis cross the strip of sand toward her, the gun dangling in the fist at his side. She was trapped.

Maddened by frustration and exertion, he strode

toward her. Alison began to dodge back and forth, to elude his grasp. After several attempts, he lunged fiercely and grabbed her arm.

Suddenly Alison saw a black shape dart across her vision. Within seconds, Trevor's voice broke into a shrill cry of pain. His arm jerked away from Alison's neck, and he dropped to his knees as the gun clattered away on the rocks. He clutched at the arm torn open by a jagged wound.

Staggering back, Alison heard a snarling noise as if from the memory of a nightmare. There, crouched a few yards away and readying for another spring, was the dead Mr. Croyden's animal, the 'seeing knife' of his vengeance. Maddened by the death of its master, it had somehow trailed Alison, the object of the last command given to it. Its primitive cunning had led it slinking aboard trains and ferries until it had picked up the scent of its prey again. It had tracked her here and had made its attack just as Trevor had grasped her. The razor teeth had found his flesh instead of hers. But now the animal had clearly sighted her and began creeping forward, its yellow eyes pinning her against her granite trap.

"Alison!" Another voice came suddenly, echoing against the cliffs. It can't be, she thought dazedly. But she turned and saw him; Eric was running across the stretch of sand toward her.

I've gone mad. People see things before they die, she told herself. But that person coming toward me in the chilling rain certainly looks real.

"The gun!" she screamed, pointing to where it lay on the rocks. "Quick!"

Eric scooped it up as he ran, both hands gripping it tightly. It was a kind unfamiliar to him, but a red dot on the side showed that the safety release was off; all that was left was to pull the trigger. Grateful for his years of varmint-shooting at home—he took aim and fired.

In mid air it suddenly jerked and twisted about. Curling in on itself, it landed in a crumpled heap of matted fur.

Eric ran past the dead animal to his sister.

"Alison!" His words rushed out. "Are you all right? What's going on?"

"The man," gasped Alison, pointing past Eric. "Stop him before he gets away."

Eric turned and saw Trevor starting up the narrow path to the face of the cliff.

Before Eric could catch up with him, he was moving out along the Bad Step. Fingers clawing for a grip, he reached up into the boulder's cracks and started inching his way slowly around it. The combination of the rain pouring over it and the animal wound on his arm were too much. He stopped halfway around, and for a moment both Alison and Eric could see his agonized, straining face. Then the fingers lost their hold upon the rock, and with a wailing cry, the figure fell backward from the stone, dropping into the freezing water below.

"Who—who was that?" demanded Eric as he ran

back to his sister. "What's going on here?"

Alison leaned against her brother's shoulder, trying to draw some of his strength into her own exhausted frame.

"Thank God you're here!" she murmured. "I prayed you'd come, but I didn't really believe you would. How did you ever know to come here?"

"The notes," said Eric, "when I got back to my lodging in Edinburgh, I found one from you saying that I should get back here to Skye as soon as I could. Your handwriting was so shaky that I was really alarmed. Then, when I got to Broadford I found you gone and a note in your room from someone named Trevor telling you to come out to the Camasunary place, and a lot of stuff about you being in some kind of danger. So I hired one of the little fishing boats there at Broadford. The note gave me the idea."

He pointed to the inlet where a small skiff with an outboard engine was pulled up on the sand.

"First, I went around the coast to Camasunary. There was nothing there, but the grass was trampled down as if there had been some kind of a fight. Then I came around the cliffs, and that's when I saw all this going on." He grabbed her by both shoulders and turned her to face him.

"What happened? Who was that man?"

"That—that man was Trevor Nevis. I'll tell you everything, but let's go."

She groaned. "And all I ever wanted were a few innocent notes from Tolstoy!"

Numbly she made her way, with Eric's steadying hand, down over the rocks to the boat. She huddled in the bow as Eric started the small outboard motor. The cold rain fell with increasing force as they moved out into the rough waters of the inlet.

After...

Before noon the next day, Broadford was forced to reverse its winter retirement. An invasion of people—almost as many as in the height of the tourist season—descended on the little town. Scotland Yard, CIA, diving teams, all kinds of experts—a KGB spy of Trevor Nevis' like was a big event. Not to mention Mr. Croyden. The discovery of his vengeance helped the authorities close haunting files on more than one continent.

Alison and Eric headed straight for the authorities after their return from the barren cove near Bad Step. Except for a hurried trip to make sure Trevor Nevis' compatriots had not closed in on Anya Savina, Alison spent the next few days going over the incredible events with the law enforcement agencies.

Eric let Alison out of his protective sight only once—to call Gramps in Washington. The first result was a freeze on any news leak of Alison Thorne's innocent involvement in the bizarre discovery. The second, the almost instant materialization of two Secret Service agents.

It was a while before Anya Savina could grasp the idea that danger had been closing in around her. When she understood Alison's intervention, she wept and held the girl to her heart.

The wife of Petros Rascomine confirmed Alison's suspicions that he had carved the dance notations on the standing stones.

"Yes," she said, "he little knew how dangerous such an act could be. I've felt for many years that the artistic value of those notations was offset by the danger they contained. The present Kazhiristan government is one of the few progressive spots of light in that dark, troubled area of the world. I knew that if the sacred dances were made public and reintroduced to Kazhiristan, the country would be plunged back into turmoil. That's why I have kept the secret of the markings on those stones for so long. Your coming here made me realize how easy it would be for the truth to leak out."

Her face was etched with deep lines of concern as she spoke.

Now it was Eric's turn to redeem himself for not being around while his sister was running for her life over the hills of Skye.

"Why not let that balmy historical enthusiast loose up there to get rid of the stones?" he suggested to his

186

surprised hearers.

"Dr. Rockingham's pamphlet describes a primitive method of destruction that worked on some Druid stones. It might just do the trick!"

"I don't know if I can handle another one of her visitations," Brother Thomas shuddered, "but the idea is sound. I will contact her at once. We must do what we can to prevent another bloodbath in Kazhiristan."

There were two questions Alison had to ask before she went back to Broadford.

"It was you, wasn't it?" she asked looking into Anya Savina's eyes. "You fired the rifle shots at me, didn't you?"

Anya Savina sighed and nodded her head sadly.

"I'm very sorry about that," she said, "but you were never in any real danger. I'm actually quite a good shot—a necessity here in the wilderness. I only wanted to scare you off for reasons you now know. I was sure you were about to discover the markings on those stones were the much sought notations."

"There's one more thing," Alison said, "and I'm not even sure I want to hear the answer. Did your husband ever mention Mr. Croyden?"

"Yes. He was one of the linguists who went to Kazhiristan with him. When my husband came back, he broke off his connection with the other linguist—I believe his name was Strother—because he had told the Bolshevik group that Croyden was working for the Kazhiristan government."

"It wasn't Petros Rascomine who told them that?"

187

Anya shook her head vigorously.

"Of course not. As a matter of fact, my husband spent a great deal of time and effort trying to trace Croyden, but it was impossible to get any information out of Russia then."

"Thank you," said Alison. "I had to know."

The road from Broadford to the dying Tolstoyan Community had become familiar to the Thorne twins before the evening they drove out for their final farewell visit.

They were not the only visitors this time. Eric parked the rented Morris Minor between two large equipment vans.

The first person they saw when they climbed the path was Dr. Rockingham.

"My dear young friends," she boomed as she came striding over to them. "I want to thank you for making all the arrangements for destroying these fake stones—"

"The idea came from your own pamphlet," Eric interrupted.

The buxom self-styled custodian of history shrugged and went on, "As you can see, the Society hired a film crew to record it. It will make a superb historical documentation—a perfect reenactment of medieval practices regarding stone monuments. This hasn't been done in Britain for centuries. Come along—they're about to topple the stone into the pit."

She turned and strode along the path to the stone

circle, Alison and Eric following her.

While a cameraman focused on them, a dozen or so men, all members of Dr. Rockingham's historical society, pulled at thick ropes strung about the tops of the tallest stone in the circle. It tilted slowly, stopped, then crashed into the deep, straw-filled pit at its base. Torches were thrown into the pit and the straw quickly caught fire, sending up a dark cloud of smoke and beginning the process of heating the stone. Barrels of water stood poised at the pit's edge, ready to pour upon the stone when it was fully heated in order to crack it into pieces.

Alison walked to the edge of the pit and looked down at the burning straw, its flames dancing around the dark stone. She pulled a manila envelope from inside her jacket. The envelopes held the negatives and the prints the photographer Trent had made of the markings upon the stones. Alison leafed through them one last time, then stuffed them back into the envelope and threw it down onto the fire. It caught quickly, curling into dark ash. The last traces of the sacred dances spiralled upward with the billowing smoke.

"We have one more appointment to keep," she told Eric as she walked away.

A crackling fire was waiting for them in the isolated cottage on the floor of the valley. A table was laid simply with immaculate white linen, silver, and centered with an antique samovar. Candles were flickering from every nook and corner.

The first clang of the bell brought Anya and Brother

Thomas from the cottage kitchen where they had been preparing the choicest dishes of rural Russia.

It was a night to remember.

After dinner they begged Anya to play for them. The great concert pianist filled the little cottage with more virtuoso than Alison and Eric dreamed possible.

"She has not played so well for many years," Brother Thomas whispered to Alison. "The fear is flowing out through her fingers—"

Later, around the fire, Anya presented them with another gift. She gave them a handwritten copy of the translation she had made of Tolstoy's letters to her father.

"They are yours to do with as you will," she said simply to Alison. "You have earned them many times over."

On such a night, when two generations and two worlds come together in such harmony, it is easy to lose track of time. The fire softened to embers and was replenished many times as Brother Thomas recounted story after story about the great author Tolstoy. Anya sat half dozing, half listening, often smiling, beside him.

At midnight, Eric nudged Alison and pointed to his watch. Reluctantly, she pulled herself back to the world of waiting Secret Service agents and travel time-tables. Quietly they gathered up the valuable letters and Anya's translations. Their movements went unnoticed by the others.

Pausing at the knotted wooden door in the hallway

before they slipped into the night, they strained their ears one more time for the voice of the aging story-teller.

"During the warm weather, the master shut down the school at Yasmaya Polyana and the pupils had to work in the fields. He himself rose at four in the morning to help his *muzhiks* with the heaviest chores.

"He wrote of those experiences; 'After sweating blood and tears, everything seemed beautiful to me—' "

"I think I know how he felt," Alison said softly as they closed the door behind them and headed up the path, filling their lungs with the pungent blend of wood smoke and hillside heather.

The *Thorne Twins* Adventure Books
by Dayle Courtney

#1—*Flight to Terror*
    Eric and Alison's airliner is shot down by terrorists over the African desert (*2713*).

#2—*Escape From Eden*
    Shipwrecked on the island of Molokai in Hawaii, Eric must escape from the Children of Eden, a colony formed by a religious cult (*2712*).

#3—*The Knife With Eyes*
    Alison searches for a priceless lost art form on the Isle of Skye in Scotland (*2716*).

#4—*The Ivy Plot*
    Eric and Alison infiltrate a Nazi organization in their hometown of Ivy, Illinois (*2714*).

#5—*Operation Doomsday*
    Lost while skiing in the Colorado Rockies, the twins uncover a plot against the U.S. nuclear defense system (*2711*).

#6—*Omen of the Flying Light*
    Staying at a ghost town in New Mexico, Eric and Alison discover a UFO and the forces that operate it (*2715*).